MYSTERY AT MORANIA

MYSTERY AT MORANIA

A Novel

Judy Conlin

iUniverse, Inc.
New York Lincoln Shanghai

Mystery at Morania
A Novel

Copyright © 2006 by Judy Conlin

iUniverse books may be ordered through booksellers or by contacting:

iUniverse
2021 Pine Lake Road, Suite 100
Lincoln, NE 68512
www.iuniverse.com
1-800-Authors (1-800-288-4677)

This is a work of fiction. All of the characters, names, incidents, organizations and dialogue in this novel are either the products of the author's imagination or are used fictitiously.

ISBN-13: 978-0-595-40440-7 (pbk)
ISBN-13: 978-0-595-84816-4 (ebk)
ISBN-10: 0-595-40440-5 (pbk)
ISBN-10: 0-595-84816-8 (ebk)

Printed in the United States of America

TO LEE

If I could find a stairway,
I'll tell you what I'd do,
I'd walk right up to heaven
And give this book to you.

CHAPTER 1

▼

Nancy heard the soft thud of earth hit the casket, though a flood of tears spared her the sight. Someone gripped her elbow and guided her stumbling toward the waiting car. The wind whipped through the cemetery lifting her long strawberry blond hair from the collar of her thin tweed coat. Chilled fingers of air stroked her neck.

Alone, alone again, she thought. The dredging up of long buried grief intensified her anguish and isolation; Grief at age ten when she waited at Grandma's. "Grandma, make them come home. I don't want Mommy and Daddy to go to heaven. Make them come home in the airplane like they promised." Grief again at age twenty-three when that little grandma, who had raised her, had a heart attack and joined her parents.

Now, at twenty-four, as she was half lifted into the car, grief surrounded her so completely she was amazed there was room for her husband's friend, Brent, to climb in beside her. Becoming both a bride and a widow in one week is something only I could do, she thought. What kind of a jinx am I? Why does everyone I love have to die?

"You okay?" Brent, who must have been the one helping her all along, was looking at her worriedly, his glasses magnifying his own reddened eyes.

"I-I guess so. How about you?" She had been so immersed in her own sorrow she hadn't, until now, given a thought to anyone else. Brent had known Greg far longer than she had, for they'd been friends since grammar school.

He merely shrugged turning his face away from her to look out the window. "It isn't far to Morania. I wonder if it's a good idea to go there."

"I suppose it's extra hard on you who have shared so much there, but I think I understand why Mrs. Moran wanted us. Since she can't spend the summer with the son she adored, she wants to surround herself with the people who also knew and loved him. All that's left of Greg are the memories each of us carries. I know I want to cling to those with all my might." Green eyes overflowing, she found it was her turn to stare out the window.

The car slowed, as she dabbed at her eyes and turned into a long tree lined driveway. Ahead, in a park-like setting was a large house that appeared luminous. As they drew closer, she realized that the shining effect was due to huge windows twelve to fifteen feet long. They reflected the cool spring sunlight making the whole house appear to glow.

Several cars from the funeral procession were pulling up into the circular drive, their passengers disembarking, and Nancy, with Brent at her side joined them.

"Just a little longer. The worst is over," Brent murmured as Mrs. Moran led them into the lovely dining room. Here, a long harvest table was heaped with food, the offerings of friends and neighbors of the Moran family.

Nancy, whose appetite was non-existent, felt lost. She watched strangers filling their plates. They smiled sympathetically in her direction, but avoided any closer contact. She stood alone in the center of the room for even Brent had abandoned her to talk to Mrs. Moran. Then, with a toss of her head that sent her golden hair flying, she straightened her shoulders and set her jaw. Deliberately, she walked to a bench in front of sliding glass doors that opened onto a beautifully landscaped terrace. At the foot of the terrace flowed the Ohio River just as Greg had described it. She had expected to see it for the first time with him. Now, he was gone and she was alone.

"So you're the enchanting Nancy?" A sad elfin face peered at her through a maze of leaves belonging to the giant philodendron on the floor by the bench.

"And you must be the enchanting Claudia?"

"How did you know?"

"No one but Greg's sister could have his same beautiful dark eyes. Besides he showed me your picture."

Rosebud pink lips curved up in a trace of a smile as the diminutive girl popped out from behind the foliage. She appeared younger than the nineteen years attributed to her by Greg. Plopping forlornly on the bench beside Nancy, she suddenly looked either shy or sly. Nancy wasn't sure which. "We didn't know he was married. We didn't even know he had a girlfriend there," she said. "We were all shocked when you called from Las Vegas." She watched Nancy intently.

"But-but-your mother—I mean she seemed to know."

"Oh mother's a great little actress. She'd never let on that Greg didn't tell her everything, but the truth is he never told her anything. It used to madden her. She says maybe you really weren't married-that maybe you're after his money. Are you?"

Nancy felt sick to her stomach, but managed to keep her composure. "What do you think, Claudia? Do I look like a fortune hunter to you?"

The young girl tilted her head to one side and looked Nancy over from head to toe. "I don't think so," she finally said softly, "even though you do seem cool enough. I bet Greg did marry you. It's just the thing he'd do to thwart Mother's plans."

"What plans? What do you mean?"

But Claudia was slipping back through the philodendron, disappearing behind a ficus tree.

My God, I can't stay here. I can never be happy in a house where I'm under suspicion. I'll see if I can keep my room at the Galt house until I can get a flight out of Louisville. I don't know where I'll go, but anywhere would be better than here. Greg, why did you have to die? You married me because you loved me. I know you did-not to spite your mother. Oh, I've got to leave. Her mind tumbling with disjointed thoughts, Nancy stood up. Her fingers twisting at the buttons of her jacket were the only outward clue to her agitated state. As she turned to leave, she saw the reason for Claudia's quick disappearing act. The last person in the world Nancy wanted to face at the moment was bearing down upon her. "Hello, Mrs. Moran", she said, shakily.

CHAPTER 2

▼

"You're older than Greg, aren't you?" The words were nonchalant but the cool gray eyes appraising her held a hint of accusation.

This is Greg's mother, Nancy told herself. She has just lost her son and been presented with a surprise daughter-in-law. I will not allow myself to be upset by her. Neither will I upset her. The woman has enough to cope with. Somehow I'll get through this-then leave. "A couple of years, yes," she answered smoothly.

"How old are you?"

"Twenty-four,"

"Greg was only twenty-one." Now the accusation was less veiled. "That 's three years difference."

"Yes, I guess it is."

"Twenty-four is rather old to be finishing college, isn't it? No offense, Dear, but most people graduate at twenty-one or two, don't they?"

"I had to leave for two years to make enough money to finance the last two."

"So money was a problem," Mrs. Moran said softly, "and what did you do to earn this money?"

"I worked as a cocktail waitress."

"A cocktail waitress?" One eyebrow rose slightly.

"A very well paying job that I kept part-time right up until I married your son. In fact that's where I met him—in the Pink Pussycat Lounge." Nancy felt her temper rising.

"But-but you're so unlike Greg, nothing like his usual friends. I don't understand what happened."

"Confidentially, I think it was the pink tights of my pussycat outfit that attracted him," Nancy snapped, then was immediately remorseful, but Mrs. Moran was not in the least offended.

"Yes, that very well could be," she said, "but what about you? Didn't you tell me you majored in journalism? You sounded so serious about it. Greg was never a serious student, you know. I guess that's why I'm so confused."

"But that's just what attracted me to him. After six years of nothing but work and study, Greg was like a refreshing breeze. He took each day as it came, enjoyed it to the fullest, and never worried about the next. He was full of charm and fun. He could always make me laugh, and he was so-so-handsome." Nancy could go no further. The thin façade of poise she'd been wearing like a suit of armor was torn away leaving in its place a sobbing wretch of a girl.

Instinctively, Mrs. Moran put her arms around her. "I know, I know," she said, adding a few tears of her own.

As soon as she could talk, Nancy blundered on. "I can't stay here either," she said. "I thought I could but I can't."

"But of course, you can, Dear. This is where you belong, and besides I need you." The gray eyes glistened with moisture. "There's so much you and I must talk about. Anyhow," she added with a touch of triumph, "I took the liberty of sending for your things and checking you out of the Galt House."

Nancy smiled wryly. "Perhaps I can stay until my plans are firmed up," she said trying not to look at the interested spectators she had failed to notice before. One dark-eyed girl could not be ignored. She stood next to Claudia; her face so swollen from crying it should have looked liked lumpy dough, but instead didn't begin to mask her striking beauty. Who is she, Nancy wondered. Obviously a relative, but I don't think Greg mentioned her to me.

"There will also be some legalities to untangle." Mrs. Moran's voice seemed several degrees lower in temperature, and her eyes were once more cool and unreadable. "So you see, it is essential that you remain here, at least for the time being. Now, let me introduce you around."

Nancy was propelled from person to person and group to group, their names and faces becoming a hopelessly confused jumble.

"Mr. and Mrs. Whitelaw, Nancy Moran. Nancy, these are our neighbors to the east. And this is John Stacy, our solicitor. John, Nancy. Greg's-uh-wife." Nancy saw Brent's familiar face and steered toward it. He was talking to Fred and Scott, the two friends who were with Greg when he died. They both said 'hello' to her, then quickly excused themselves.

Nancy watched their backs disappearing through the crowd. "What have I got-the plague?" She tried for a light touch but didn't quite make it.

Brent smiled. "I think you'll find a lot of people uncomfortable with you right now. What do you say to a bride who just lost her husband? And most of these people are trying to deal with their own feelings as well. Everyone is still in shock. They have a lot to assimilate, and remember, they've had even less time than you to take it all in. Furthermore, the way Greg died has to be a source of embarrassment and gossip." Brent, himself, looked a little embarrassed.

"Surely, no one blames me?"

"Of course not." The answer came too quickly to satisfy Nancy. She searched the face of this tall skinny blonde friend of Greg's, but he was frowning. Following his gaze, she saw Claudia with the sorrowful black-eyed beauty in tow, approaching determinedly.

"I'd like you to meet Rosa," she said as a hush fell over the room. Raising the girl's left hand so that Nancy couldn't miss its significance, she added, "Greg's fiancée."

CHAPTER 3

▼

The gaudy gem held Nancy mesmerized for a moment. Her own finger, naked except for a slim gold band, seemed inferior next to this perfectly manicured and apparently lovingly adorned digit. Summoning will power she didn't know she had, she clasped that left hand in both of her own.

"How do you do, Rosa?" she said adding the lie loudly enough so that everyone could hear. "I've heard so much about you." Still smiling politely, she turned nodding to those on her left and right and walked majestically through the sliding glass doors.

She held the posture until she could no longer be seen from any of the huge windows, which meant she had to make a wide arc through the fringe of trees down over the bank toward the river. With the boathouse between her and the main house, she abandoned her controlled posture and allowed great sobs to shake her body. Leaning against the boathouse, she wept until exhausted, then sank to the ground with her back against the structure and looked out across the river.

Six weeks earlier, about the middle of April, she and Greg had been looking across another river, the Raritan in New Brunswick, New Jersey. She had met him the night before in the Pink Pussycat....

"Here kitty kitty. Here kitty kitty."

Nancy was used to dealing with such advances. Every night some customer tried the same or a similar line. Tonight she glanced at the table from which the baiting emanated. There were two of the usual Rutger's rowdies, slightly inebriated and very pleased with their brand of humor, ogling her. It was the third member of the party who surprised her, however. Neater and better dressed than the other two, he seemed to be enjoying the show they were putting on while not becoming actively involved himself, and when he saw her looking in his direction, he gave her the sweetest smile.

"Here kitty kitty. Why don't you come over here? We'd like to pet you." Raucous laughter. The two were becoming obnoxious.

"There are a couple of cats in here who are about to be put out for the night," she warned jerking her head in the bouncer's direction.

Chester flexed his muscles on cue, and the trio finished their drinks and left shortly with no further remarks in Nancy's direction.

At closing time she was waiting for Chester to walk her to the bus stop, as was their usual routine, when a shiny red corvette pulled up beside her.

"Want a lift?" It was the owner of that disarming smile and he was flashing another one her way.

"I take the bus, thank you."

"And you're not about to get in a car with a stranger? Tell you what. We'll take the Hulk with us", (here he pointed at Chester who was just emerging), "and I'll drop you first, then him. That way you'll be perfectly safe. By the way I'm Greg Moran."

And that's the way it happened except for one thing. After being dropped off, Nancy was preparing for bed when there was a knock on her dorm door.

"Who is it?"

"Greg."

"How did you get in?" Nancy knew that all the outside doors to the dormitories were kept locked for security reasons. Each student got two keys, one for the outside door to his building and one for his room.

"I live in twenty-eight which is connected by tunnel, the same building Chester lives in. I recognized him from seeing him around. He's hard to miss, you know?"

"Clever. What do you want?" She opened the door a crack and his handsome open boyish face peeped in.

"I want to see you tomorrow, all day."

"I have classes."

"Cut them."

"I can't."

"You can. Pick you up at eight." He pulled the door back closed.

Of course she wouldn't do it. But she did. They spent the entire day on a campus made beautiful by spring weather, foliage and flowers. They bought hot dogs and sat on the banks of the Raritan and talked about nothing important. By the end of the day, Nancy knew she was head over heels in love.

"I think they're looking for you. Want to give yourself up?"

Nancy was startled from her thoughts. She recognized Greg's dad though they'd been little more than introduced.

"Or if you'd like to make a break for it, I think the best get-a-way would be by sea. Makes it harder for the bloodhounds to pick up your scent." He was standing on the dock, a short but broad shouldered man, with a trace of a smile on his thin lips "What's your pleasure?"

With the sound of voices approaching, Nancy jumped up. "Let's go for it," she said.

Taking her by the arm, Mr. Moran guided her into a small boat. He gunned the outboard motor, which sent them roaring down the river. Neither of them spoke. Nancy faced directly into the wind enjoying the sensation of her hair streaming out behind her. If only the breeze could blow my troubles away as easily, she thought.

"The Louisville Belle," Mr. Moran said pointing to an old fashioned paddle boat on the horizon. Music and laughter drifted back to them. And, somehow, it was cheering to know there were still happy people in the world. Looking at the Louisville skyline, she could make out the revolving bar at the top of the Galt House, the hotel she had stayed at on the river. People were standing at the rail of the courtyard where she had stood the night before. She waved to them as Mr. Moran turned their small craft around to head back from whence they had come.

"The river helps put things in perspective," Mr. Moran said as they neared the boathouse. "It clears the cobwebs out. You can use the boat anytime you feel the need to get away."

Nancy felt a rush of gratitude toward this man who was Greg's father, and sought a way to tell him so as they were tying up, but, Mr. Moran finished quickly and walked away saying only, "All this will pass away, and when all is said and done, you'll find it's best that he's dead."

Nancy stood alone feeling cold all over. Could she possibly have heard correctly?

CHAPTER 4

▼

Reentering the house was not the dreaded ordeal Nancy expected. The dining room was empty, as was the long table except for a single basket of cut flowers, which replaced the former bounteous food offerings.

Unsure of where she should go, Nancy peeped into the next room. Mrs. Moran was lying on a blue sofa, a washcloth across her forehead. Nancy was about to withdraw when Mrs. Moran opened one eye. "Straight up the stairs, second door on the left," she said. "Dinner will be at six."

Following these directions, Nancy found herself outside the indicated room in a matter of minutes. She hesitated before opening the door. What if this was Greg's room? Was she up to that? She gulped, then reached out and turned the knob. She entered a feminine room done in lilac and white which showed no signs of a previous occupant. A guestroom, she decided, breathing a silent thank you to Mrs. Moran. For the moment, she forgave the woman's highhanded manner in having her bags removed from the Galt House and placed neatly beside this bed.

Refusing to think about staying for an extended period of time, she unpacked only a few things. She hung her toothbrush in the adjoining bath and laid her Rutger's snoopy nightshirt, along with Greg's old robe, across the foot of the bed. She placed portfolio, paper, and pen on the bedside stand, her make-up on the dressing table, and a few items of clothing she hoped were suitable in the bureau and wardrobe.

Her housekeeping chores done, she took a quick shower, wrapped herself in Greg's robe which still carried the faint fragrance of his aftershave, and sat on the bed, her chin resting on her knees. The terrible emptiness inside her was joined by a gnawing doubt concerning her relationship with her husband. The open shared experience she believed it to be did not seem compatible with the omission of any mention of Rosa.

Instinctively, she reached for paper and pen. Writing always made things clearer. Since childhood, whenever she was troubled, she would sort things out through the catharsis of longhand jottings in spiral bound notebooks. In college she sometimes didn't verbalize well with her professors, but when she turned in her papers, they invariably returned with A+ grades.

At the top of her paper she now wrote:

PROBLEMS

1. Why didn't Greg tell me about Rosa?

2. Why hadn't he told his family about her?

3. What plans was Claudia hinting that Mrs. Moran had for her son?

4. Why do Scott and Fred seem to want to avoid me?

5. Why would Greg's own father suggest that his death was somehow beneficial?

6. What legal entanglements could possibly involve me?

She looked over her list. It no longer seemed ominous, reduced as it was to six simple questions. Brent's explanation regarding the attitudes of Greg's friends towards her was sensible. Mr. Moran may have been trying to make the tragedy appear less so as a way of dealing with his own grief. Mrs. Moran would have plans for her son. Any mother would. Nothing sinister about that. Death always left some legal questions. Number one and two remained unanswered and she felt the answer to both of them might have been simply lack of time, for she and Greg had truly had a whirlwind romance.

They saw each other every day after that first time. Not that they were inseparable or hung on each other. Nancy would have hated that. Still, they managed to spend a part of each day together. Sometimes, Nancy would be banging away at her typewriter, while Greg lay on her cot listening to a Billy Joel album blaring away on the stereo. Other times he'd accompany her to the library or meet her for lunch.

He never seemed to study. When he wasn't in class (and that was a lot of the time, for he wasn't taking many, and those he did take, he frequently cut), he spent with Nancy and a strange assortment of buddies. He loved the campus camaraderie and hung out with all types. He might be with Calvin, a 4-0 engineering student on the College Avenue Campus with whom he enjoyed matching wits, or with some of the radicals down at the Medium, the college paper of which Nancy was managing editor, or with Scott and Fred at a beer blast or pot party.

No matter whom he was with, he enjoyed himself immensely, fitting into the group without ever becoming one of them. He could drink himself into a stupor, (which he frequently did) and awaken with such a look of innocence; Nancy could never find it in her heart to scold him.

When Nancy was free, they played miniature golf, rode bicycles, jogged, hung out in the lounge, and necked liked high school kids. When she had to work at the Pink Pussycat, he faithfully arrived to take her to and from the job though his alcohol level often mandated that she do the driving.

One day after they'd been seeing each other for about a month, he said, "I'm going to marry you the day after school is out. Okay?"

"In two weeks? You crazy or something?" she asked, tweaking his nose.

"We're flying to Las Vegas," he said handing her two tickets. "No blood tests, no waiting, and a great place for a honeymoon. Besides," he added giving her his lopsided grin, "since marriage is the biggest gamble of all, why shouldn't it take place in the biggest gambling town? Whataya say?"

"No dice is the obvious answer," Nancy grinned back, "but I think I'll take a chance." They fell into each other's arms so violently they tipped over in the grass.

"Roll again, Dealer?" Nancy giggled.

BEEP. BEEP. BEEP. It was the stupid alarm clock, which she'd set for five thirty. Quickly she threw on a beige dress and heels and ran a comb through her hair. Before she had her lipstick on, there was a knock on the door.

"Yes," she called out.

The door opened and Claudia stuck her head in. "Just wanted to make sure you were ready," she said. "Couldn't have you miss the secret plans Mama has for you tonight."

Before Nancy could respond, the door quietly reclosed.

CHAPTER 5

▼

It was a somber group at dinner, with no one really making an effort to keep the mood upbeat. Mr. Moran sat at one end of the long table, his wife at the other. Arranged along one side were Brent, Fred, Scott, and a handsome mustached man that Nancy recognized as the lawyer, John Stacy. Claudia, Rosa, and a mousy young girl, along with Nancy made up the opposite side. They sat in their self-imposed segregated by sex groups and picked at their food.

During the course of the meal, Nancy learned that the girl next to her was Melinda, a cousin of Greg's; that the rest of the relatives were eating at the Captain's Quarters, a river restaurant owned by the former governor of Kentucky, but would be stopping by later; and that Mrs. Moran's first name was Isabel. Other than that, there was little information to be gleaned. By the time the dessert was served what little conversation there was had run down like the eighth day of a seven day clock. Melinda, the least likely member of the group, was the first to try and remedy the situation.

"Uncle Ben, I saw horses and buggies on the streets of Louisville yesterday. I swear I don't recall seeing any before. Are they something new?"

Mr. Moran blinked, then nodded. "Last couple of years," he said and there was a pause for so long it seemed the topic had ended. Then, seeming to realize he had a duty to keep the ball rolling, he continued, "matter of fact, there are two different outfits operating. Guess they had quite a tussle at first with the city fathers. Worried about droppings in the street, they were. Interesting arrangement they came up with. They call it a diaper, but it's more like a trough. The horse lets go, and PLOP, it falls in the trough. The driver whisks out his deodorant spray, then between tourist runs takes care of the mess." He beamed at them all.

"Benjamin," Mrs. Moran gasped, "not at the table."

"Just the workings of nature, Woman. You don't suppose I've said anything these people have never heard of before, do you?" Nancy stifled an impulse to giggle.

"A problem of sanitation and environmental control that our forefathers didn't have to grapple with," John said solemnly, then turned to a safer subject. "Heard that Churchill Downs is in a bit of trouble financially."

"That's hard to believe," Mr. Moran said. "Plenty of people there any day the track is running."

The male side of the table came alive and was soon discussing Kentucky Derbys of the past and some of the famous horseflesh bred and raced in Kentucky.

Claudia leaned towards her mother. "When are you going to show her?" she asked in a loud whisper.

Mrs. Moran glared at her. Gracefully, she rose from her chair, tapped her water glass with a spoon and announced, "After dinner drinks will be served on the terrace."

As they filed through the glass doors, Nancy maneuvered herself into a position next to Brent. She wanted both to put some distance between herself and the malevolent stares of Rosa and to somehow manage a private conversation with Brent. No sooner were they seated on some of the gaily striped lawn furniture that dotted the terrace and tree shaded lawn, however, than they were joined by a confusing array of Greg's aunts, uncles, cousins and grandparents.

The inconsequential, inane conversation, while probably engaged in through the kindest of motives, angered Nancy. The sight of Fred and Scott slugging down their drinks and laughing together angered her still more. It made her think of their part in Greg's totally unnecessary death.

She and Greg were lying on the large queen sized bed in their room at The Hacienda, a casino a bit removed from the center of the Vegas Strip. A quieter place for a honeymoon was Greg's explanation for his choice.

This was Friday. They had checked in on Monday, asked the bellhop for directions to City Hall, gone there directly and gotten their marriage license. They were directed across the street to another city building where someone (Nancy wasn't sure of his title) jovially read the ceremony. Fifteen minutes later they walked out as man and wife. It didn't seem real.

The five days had flown in a haze of mornings spent sightseeing at Hoover Dam and Lake Mead, evenings of great food, entertainment, and slot machines, and blissful nights spent entwined in each other's arms. The rest of the world was non-existent to the two of them, lost as they were in discovering each other.

Therefore, on Friday as they lay on the bed discussing what they were going to do on this their last night in Vegas, the ringing of the phone was an unwelcome intrusion. A startled Greg answered. "Hello....Who? Scott?...Where are you?.. In Vegas. No kidding. Fred too?.... No, we're flying out in the morning."

Nancy listened to the one-sided conversation.

"Tonight? Well, Nance and I were planning on a big bash on our last night.... No, I don't think so. She's not really a partier."

"What do they want?" *Nancy interrupted signaling for him to cover the mouthpiece.*

"They want us to meet them for drinks at the Sahara."

"You go. We'll have a late dinner. I can do my hair and nails."

"But it's our honeymoon."

"Go ahead. They can have you for a little while 'cause I'll have you for the rest of our lives."

He grinned. "Okay, I'll meet you guys," *he said into the phone,* "but only for a couple of drinks."

After he was gone, Nancy washed and dried her hair, then brushed it until it gleamed. The curling iron turned it into a tamed tawny mane. She attacked toenails and fingernails with clippers, file, and cream, then painted them most appropriately with a polish called Bride's Blush. A pale green silk dress and open-toed shoes, which showed off her pedicure, completed her ensemble. With nothing left to do, she went to the gift shop and purchased some magazines.

The evening dragged and Greg did not return. By eight o'clock she was worried, by nine, angry and by ten panicky. At midnight the phone rang. It was Scott. They had gotten carried away celebrating, he said, one marriage toast leading to another, one bar leading to another.

"Where is he?" *Nancy asked wryly imagining his condition.*

Scott sounded scared. They had challenged Greg's drinking prowess, he continued, with the result that Greg tipped up a fifth of bourbon and drank the whole thing non-stop.

"My God, what happened to him?" *Fright replaced the amused tolerance Scott's first explanations had brought about.*

"He—he collapsed. He wasn't breathing. We called an ambulance."

"Where did it take him?"

Scott named the hospital adding that Fred had ridden along with him.
Nancy tore to the hospital only to find that Greg had been dead on arrival.

"Nancy, Nancy," Mrs. Moran was standing beside her on the terrace. "Didn't you hear me? I said I wanted to show you something."

CHAPTER 6

▼

Numbly, Nancy followed Mrs. Moran back into the house to a small office.

"Sit down, Dear," Mrs. Moran said pointing to a beanbag chair as she walked over and picked up a postcard from the lady's desk in the corner. "What do you make of this?" she asked, thrusting the card forward.

Nancy's hand trembled as she reached for it; for there could be no doubt that the writing was Greg's unique, almost illegible, scrawl. She studied the Las Vegas postmark. It had been mailed Wednesday, two days before he died. She turned it over and looked at a picture of the Hacienda. She had seen identical postcards in the desk drawer of their room there, but she hadn't known Greg had sent any.

"Aren't you going to read it?" Mrs. Moran grabbed the card, flipped it, and returned it to Nancy's bloodless fingers so quickly it was hard to believe it had happened.

The message was short:

DEAR MOM AND DAD,

DECIDED TO TAKE A BREAK IN VEGAS AFTER THE TOUGH COLLEGE GRIND TO UNWIND BEFORE COMING HOME. HAVEN'T LOST TOO MUCH MONEY, IN FACT WON ONE BIG JACKPOT. TELL THE BRAT

(CLAUDIA) AND ROSA NOT TO WORRY. HANDSOME ADORABLE GREG WILL SOON BE THERE.

LOVE,

GREG

P.S. INTEND TO SKIP GRADUATION CEREMONIES. SORRY, MOM. HOPE YOU DIDN'T MAKE ELABORATE PLANS. G.

Nancy read it over twice. There was not one mention of her or their marriage. "When did you get this?" she finally asked.

"Saturday."

After she talked to me on the phone Friday night, Nancy thought, but said nothing.

"Well, what do you make of it?" Mrs. Moran prompted.

Trying to hide her hurt and confusion, Nancy turned to the older woman. "I didn't know he hit a jackpot," was all she could think of to say.

Mrs. Moran's reaction was unexpected. "I'm afraid you'll have to come up with something better than that," she snapped and marched out of the room leaving Nancy alone.

"I don't understand," Nancy protested, but there was no one to hear her. She allowed herself another crying bout, then returned to her room to repair the damage before presenting herself once more on the terrace. This time Brent was standing alone down by the river and Nancy determinedly joined him.

"Tell me about Greg and Rosa," she commanded without preamble.

Brent remained unperturbed. "What do you want to know?"

"Everything."

"I'll tell you what I can. Rosa is Rosa Whitelaw, daughter of the Whitelaws who live on the estate to the east of Morania. Morania, by the way, is only the summer home of the Morans. They spend most of the year at their condo in the city. Rosa's been in love with Greg since they were children, but Greg always treated her much as he does Claudia—like a little sister. Mrs. Moran has always tried to make more of the relationship, engineering Greg into taking Rosa to dances, movies and so on."

"And would Greg do it? Nancy couldn't imagine him being so easily maneuvered.

"Sometimes, yes. Sometimes, no. Most of the outings I know about involved both Claudia and Rosa, although he did take Rosa to her senior prom." He stopped talking and gazed once more across the river.

"But, what about an engagement? When and how did that come about?"

Brent peered at her solemnly through his glasses. "Believe me," he said, his voice full of hurt, "you know as much about that as I do."

Nancy suddenly realized how little she knew this friend of Greg's. They had met at Spring Fest at Rutgers, when he had visited Greg. She hadn't seen him again until three days ago. As soon as he'd learned of Greg's death from the Moran's, he'd flown to Vegas and become Nancy's strength, taking over many of the troublesome details. He made the arrangements for the body to be flown to Kentucky, and made reservations for Nancy at the Galt House. He packed clothes, saw that Nancy was exposed to meals even if she didn't eat, and took care of checking her out of the Hacienda and getting the two of them to the airport.

"You mean you don't know about the engagement?" Nancy couldn't help feeling glad. She had wondered why he hadn't prepared her. Maybe the whole thing was something Claudia made up, she thought hopefully.

Again, a strange pained expression flitted across his fair features. "No. I had no idea." His voice cracked a little and his eyes didn't look at Nancy this time, but instead were focused far across the lawn.

Turning to follow his gaze, Nancy saw Fred walking toward the swimming pool, his arm around a voluptuous Rosa, clad only in a bright pink bikini. Could Brent be falling for Rosa, she wondered. Before she could give this new idea further thought, she saw John Stacy walking purposefully toward her, a stern look upon his face.

CHAPTER 7

▼

"Excuse me," John Stacy said to Brent, "but I'd like to talk to Miss-er Mrs. Moran for a few minutes."

Brent seemed only too pleased to escape, though he did manage a smile and a wave. "Catch ya later," he said to Nancy and went off in the general direction of the pool.

"Is the Moran's pool heated?" Nancy asked John trying to reconcile Rosa's bikini and the cool spring evening weather.

The faint smile that flickered across his stone face before it settled back into its former expression made Nancy aware of how stupid her question must have sounded to him. "As a matter of fact, it is" he said, "but before you think of taking a dip, I'd like to talk seriously to you."

"What about?"

"I don't know if you remember or not, but I am the Moran's lawyer, and as such, need to take care of some legal matters involving you."

"Like what?"

"I know you are exhausted tonight, but tomorrow I promise to sit down with you and go over several matters that need clarification."

He's very handsome, Nancy thought, but such a stuffed shirt. "Like what?" she again demanded, hoping to find out what in the world he was trying to tell her.

"When a death occurs, there is always the question of wills and inheritance, the disposal of property and personal possessions."

Nancy couldn't help laughing. "I realize the Morans are well to do, "she interrupted, "but the only things of value Greg had were his stereo, his corvette, and a

Maxi Teller checking account that he was always trying to draw more out of than he put in."

John Stacy did not laugh. "Nevertheless I've taken the liberty of setting up an appointment to meet and discuss these matters with you tomorrow morning at nine sharp. I would prefer to meet in my own office but Mrs. Moran has requested that I remain here. Therefore, I have reserved the use of the library for that time."

It took an effort to refrain from the laughter his pomposity evoked. Imagine someone reserving the library in a private home. She managed to say, "That will be very satisfactory," without sounding sarcastic.

"And now Mrs. er uh," he ground to a halt, a faint blush on his cheeks that made him appear more personable.

"Call me Nancy," she said in a kinder tone.

"Nancy," he said, haltingly. "Nancy, if you'd like, I could escort you over to that pool you expressed an interest in."

"If you're sure it's ethical," Nancy replied impishly. "After all we will be on opposite sides of the table tomorrow, (or will it be a desk?) when we discuss the disposal of the probably negative balance in Greg's account."

John Stacy's pale brown eyes were full of disapproval. "This is nothing to joke about," he said. "In view of the recent bereavement of this family, and I should think, of yourself, your flip attitude is out of place and out of order."

Not wanting him to know how much his rebuke hurt, Nancy blinked back the threatened tears. "I think I'll forego that trip to the pool, Mr. Stacy," she said. "Goodnight." She turned her back on him and walked toward the boathouse.

"Thinking of making a break for it again?" Mr. Moran must spend all time puttering around the boathouse.

"Some things you can't run away from," Nancy answered trying hard to pull herself together.

"Some things or some people?" Mr. Moran wiped his greasy hands on an old rag as he sat on the overturned pail and motioned Nancy towards another. "Saw that ambulance chaser with you. What did he want?"

Nancy didn't feel her dress and heels appropriate to the seating arrangement, so she remained standing. "Nothing in particular," she said not wishing to repeat their conversation and her humiliation.

"He's a nice enough lad. Ambitious. Gonna amount to something. Too bad Greg couldn't have been more like him."

"Greg was better in every way than that-that pompous jerk," Nancy retorted. "How can you say such a thing?"

"Everyone's entitled to his opinion," he said mildly, "but don't forget, I knew him longer."

"I think I'll go in," Nancy said. "It's been a long hard day."

"Seems there are some things and people you can run away from," Mr. Moran called after her, "at least temporarily."

Nancy made a wide arc around the grounds in an effort to avoid the clusters of people that seemed to be everywhere. She had almost reached the house, when she found her way blocked by a plump blond woman.

"Oh, my Dear, I am sooo sorry for you. To lose your poor husband after only one week. It's just tooooo tragic." She didn't look like a predator-rather pretty, in fact, in a blue silk dress with a large floppy hat to match. Nevertheless, Nancy felt like a mouse being played with by a cat. "I'm Greg's Aunt Tessie. To think that he actually drank himself to death. Unbelievable. And how awful for a pretty little thing like you."

Nancy nodded and murmured, "yes, it was." She darted around the woman and into the house, not stopping until she was safely in her room with the door locked between her and the rest of the world.

After she put on her snoopy nightshirt, she brushed her teeth and hair, creamed her face, and took two of the sleeping pills the doctor had given her at the hospital in Las Vegas. Before going to bed, she slipped on the large robe and slipped out on the balcony adjoining her room. It was much nicer up here looking out over the pool and river, watching all those people who made her so uncomfortable up close while she was unobserved herself. She felt as safe and secure up here as she had anywhere since she had discovered a world that allowed this to happen to her Greg.

Turning to go back inside, she saw the curtain on the door lift at the bottom left corner. There was no breeze and the curtain was fastened on a rod both top and bottom. Maybe she was wrong. No, there it was again being lifted on the other side as if someone was trying to peek out at her. Her heart was galloping along at an alarming rate, and it sounded as though it was outside rather than inside her body.

Had she locked someone in that room with her? The balcony no longer was the haven it had formerly appeared to be. She felt vulnerable and exposed.

She took a deep breath and gripped the doorknob with both hands so tightly her knuckles shown white in the twilight. Slowly, she pushed the door open.

CHAPTER 8

▼

Nancy peered into the widening slice of darkness revealed by the increasing angle of the opening door, and wished she had left a lamp on. Although she was frightened, the shock and depression of the last few days had left her in a state where she merely wanted to face whatever or whoever awaited her and get it over with. She could see nothing, however.

"Anyone there?" she asked. No answer, only a soft rustling sound.

Tentatively, she stepped into the room with her right foot, while her hand on that side felt along the wall looking for the light switch. Why hadn't she thought to locate it earlier? What was that? She had bumped into the bureau and there was a plop onto the floor. Something touched her foot, something soft and alive. She stiffened, her muscles growing taut and she felt goosebumps on her arms. Her hand felt what it had been searching for at the same time a low rumbling sound began to fill the room.

Her muscles relaxed, as she flicked the switch on for she recognized that sound. "Hi there," she said looking down at the small face turned up to her. "Who are you?"

"Purr," was all the yellow cat replied as it rubbed around the robe at her ankles.

Nancy laughed. "So it was you sitting on the bureau, pulling at the curtain? You rascal, you. You certainly gave me a fright."

She bent down and picked up the small creature, which she carried over to the bed. It cuddled down beside her as she read over the questions in her journal, and was soon asleep. Nancy, too, felt drowsy as the sleeping tablets began to take effect. She pulled back the top linen taking care not to dislodge the yellow ball of fur with the black mark on its nose. Before she could crawl into bed, however, there was a knock on the door. Drat, what now?

Who is it?" she asked.

"Claudia".

With a sigh she unlocked the door and let Greg's sister in. Claudia walked over to sit on the bed, and the yellow cat jumped to its feet, hissing and arching its back before disappearing under the bed.

Claudia watched open-mouthed. "How did you ever get Shammy in here?"

"Shammy? So that's his name?"

"Her name. Shammy's a girl, but she's not noted for her sociability. The only one she ever had anything to do with was Greg. How did you get her to accept you, to be so tame?"

"I had nothing to do with it. She came in when I wasn't here and made herself at home. Was she Greg's?"

"Yes, he brought her home one day—said someone must have dropped her off. He named her Chameleon; because she seems to blend in with the surroundings so completely she becomes invisible. That got shortened to Shammy."

"What do you mean she's not sociable?"

"You saw how she hissed and ran under the bed. She wasn't like that with Greg. He carried her on his shoulder; she slept with him and followed him everywhere. When he wasn't here, she had nothing to do with the rest of us, just kept hidden. We'd forget she was here except her food bowl gets emptied, and we see her slinking around occasionally. You know," she continued touching Greg's robe, "I bet this is what attracted her."

"There's so much I never had a chance to learn about Greg," Nancy said sadly.

"Or that he didn't want you to learn." Claudia again flashed that rather sly grin. "Like about Rosa."

"I've been thinking about Rosa. Something must have changed between them, something that you didn't know anything about. I'm sure he wouldn't have married me otherwise."

"Did you read the postcard Mother got? Didn't sound like anything changed to me."

"Why are you here? Do you want anything in particular?" Nancy tried to take charge of the conversation, but a yawn spoiled her assertiveness. She was getting very sleepy.

"I just wanted to warn you to be careful tomorrow."

"To be careful? Why?"

"John Stacy is very clever."

Nancy forced herself to concentrate on Claudia's words. Fighting to keep her eyes open, she asked, "But why must I be careful?"

"He's also ruthless," the small girl sitting on her bed said conspiratorially. Before she could elaborate further, there was another knock on the door. Claudia jumped up guiltily, then seemed to compose herself. "Want me to get that?" she asked.

Nancy nodded.

Claudia opened the door. Rosa stood outside; her bikini apparently covered by a long multi-colored robe for its hood didn't conceal several tendrils of dripping wet hair around the beautiful face that looked out beneath it. Her chattering teeth were another indication that she'd just come from the pool.

"What are you doing here?" Claudia asked accusingly.

"And I might ask the same of you," Rosa retorted, black eyes snapping.

"Girls, I took some sleeping pills and I just can't keep awake. Please can't we talk tomorrow?"

"I guess so," the shivering Rosa said slowly, though she looked a little sullen.

"Of course." Claudia looked relieved as she pulled the door closed behind her. Then she stuck her head back in. "Remember what I said though," she whispered.

The warning made a chill run down Nancy's spine as she crawled into bed at last. She felt so alone in this house with these strangers and their emotional innuendoes. She felt so alone in this bed without the sweet warmth of Greg's body. But suddenly she wasn't alone. Shammy's warm little body curled up in the curve of her arm as if the cat knew they were both missing the same person. Together they fell asleep.

CHAPTER 9

▼

A small yellow and white paw patted Nancy's eyelids and nose. She didn't want to wake up, but the patting was insistent. Her mouth was dry and ugly tasting from the sleeping pills, and her limbs heavy and difficult to move. She felt the way slow motion looked on TV.

"Okay, Shammy. Okay," she said, as the cat sat on her chest purring and patting intermittently. She forced here eyes open. Once focussed, she realized she'd overslept. Her appointment with John Stacy was at nine and here it was, already eight fifteen. "Guess you must be able to tell time," she told her feline friend, who merely jumped off the bed as if off duty, and nonchalantly strolled to the door. Nancy, whose mind was busily sorting through her wardrobe for the appropriate attire for this meeting, absently opened the door.

"Gosh, you're going to be late." Claudia was rocketing down the hall wearing bib overalls, her hair in braids, tied with bright red ribbons, and a tennis racket in her hand which she waved in Nancy's direction.

"You're right," Nancy said and firmly closed the door as soon as Shammy's tail was safely on the other side. She didn't feel like verbally jousting with Greg's sister this morning.

A quick shower helped counteract the effect of the sleeping pills, and Nancy's spirits began to rise. She put on a pale green linen suit, a little makeup, and a pair of comfortable shoes. How Greg had liked this outfit. "Makes your eyes glow like cat's eyes," he'd said. Was he thinking of Shammy? she wondered. Why hadn't he told her about his cat? There were so many things she wanted to know and now could never ask him. The enormity of her loss overwhelmed her, and for a moment she stood, head bowed, immersed in her grief once more. Shaking her head to dispel such thoughts, she hurried downstairs, hoping for at least a cup of coffee to compose herself before her meeting.

She found juice, coffee, and a sweet roll, which she gulped down quickly, the necessity for haste coming to her aid in her struggle to get a hold on her emotions. Even so, by her watch, she was ten minutes late as she hurried to the library.

John Stacy's glance at his own watch, as Nancy rushed into the room was enough to immediately put her on the defensive. Who did he think he was anyhow? John's first words answered this unspoken question, "I am the Moran's lawyer," he said without preamble, "and, as such, am here to act solely and exclusively on their behalf. Do you understand?" He looked up from the stack of papers he was shuffling and imperiously waved his hand. The gesture, Nancy assumed, meant he wished her to be seated in that uncomfortable chair in front of the table behind which he was standing.

She nodded her head and obediently sat down, while John lowered himself into the chair across from her. Clearing his throat and once more beginning his paper shuffling, he began speaking in a low voice, his gaze fixed somewhere near Nancy's chair.

"Your-ah-er-Greg appears to have died intestate," he began slowly. "The order in which property is passed to the various blood relatives" (his voice gave a slight emphasis to the words blood relatives) "upon the death of its owner without a will demands the application of the rules of the statutes of each state. There is, however, a general scheme followed by all these statutes. Interestingly enough," he smiled and moved his eyes up to Nancy's, a bit of animation creeping into his monotonous lawyer tone, "it parallels pretty closely the ancient rules of English sovereign lines of succession."

"I'm sure this is all very interesting," Nancy interrupted, "but just what does all this have to do with me? I take it by your subtle emphasis that a wife is not a blood relative, so what are you trying to say?"

"A wife is not a blood relative." John was once more gazing at her chin. "In fact, a wife is never the heir to her husband, legally speaking. Only a blood relative can be an heir in the traditional sense of the law. The wife's position, however, has been improved by today's tendency toward equal rights. A typical statute, as in Kentucky, provides that if the deceased leaves a surviving spouse and no issue, one half of the estate goes to the spouse and one half to the parents in equal shares. If either parent is dead, his portion-"

"Wait a minute." Again Nancy interrupted. "You keep going on and on. What does this have to do with me?" Her journalistic mind had to get to the bottom line. "Greg was just out of college. He had no major property, so what it is you wish to tell me?"

John Stacy squirmed in his chair. His cheeks appeared flushed, as his hands nervously shuffled. "Before we discuss property, legally we must have proof that you were married to Greg. So far we have only your word. I'm sure-"

"I see." Nancy said, coldly. "Our marriage certificate should be proof enough." She walked haughtily from the room. Once outside, she found she was shaking from suppressed anger, but she was determined not to show it. She hastened upstairs.

She was surprised to find Shammy once more in her room, but the little cat's presence did help to calm her. "You little scamp," she said. "Can you turn doorknobs as well as tell time?" When she went to get her briefcase, she found it not as she'd left it. It was tipped over, its contents spilling onto the floor. "And I suppose you knew what I was after, too, and were just about to get it for me?" She laughed and tickled the cat under her chin. "What a scamp you are," she said bending down and pricking up the papers, but search as she would; her marriage certificate was no longer where she'd placed it.

CHAPTER 10

▼

"Where ya been? Out in the boat?" Nancy was munching a sandwich at one of the umbrella tables and watching Brent approaching via the path from the river.

'No, not me. I hate boats," he said hastily. "I-I was just walking."

"I thought I saw Mr. Moran's hat bobbing around down by the boathouse. Did you see him?"

"No. No, I didn't."

"Sit down with me. I'll share if you don't mind peanut butter and jelly". Brent grinned and accepted the offer. "And what have you been up to?" he asked.

Nancy told him about her meeting with John Stacy and about the missing certificate.

"There certainly has to be a record of your marriage in Las Vegas, and the certificate can easily be replaced," he said logically. "It may not have been in your briefcase at all. Remember we left in a rush."

"What does it really matter?" Nancy asked. "Greg didn't have all that much to leave anyhow, did he?"

But Brent wasn't listening. His eyes were riveted on Rosa coming up the same path he had just traversed. Today she looked the image of a Southern Belle in a white sundress that accentuated her tiny waist before billowing out into a full skirt strewn with tiny red bows. The white of her sandals and sundress set off the attractive tan of her skin. Brent appeared mesmerized as he stumbled to his feet and held out a chair for her.

She sat down ignoring Brent and turning to Nancy. "I need to talk to you," she said.

"Talk away," Nancy said remembering that Rosa had come to her room before and had been sent away, "but I must warn you. I can't stay long. I have to find a certain young lawyer and teach him the fundamentals of searching for evidence."

Neither Brent nor Rosa smiled at her attempt at sarcastic humor.

"Later-alone-when you have time," Rosa said, "but please don't forget."

"Okay," Nancy said, and then as a silence settled over the trio, she decided that maybe three was a crowd, so she excused herself.

She slid the screen of the sliding glass doors silently open and stepped inside, pausing for a moment to allow her eyes a chance to adjust to the sudden dimness after the brilliant sunlight outdoors.

"Well, did she have any proof of a marriage to Greg?" Isabelle Moran was standing with her back to Nancy just beyond the miniature jungle of giant philo-dendrons, schefflera, ficus trees, and hanging plants that almost covered the wide expanse of glass.

Startled, Nancy stood where she was, then realized that by hesitating she had lost the chance to enter the room naturally. Now she would cause embarrass-ment, and probably they would think she'd been deliberately eavesdropping. There was nothing to do but crouch where she was, and hope they'd go before someone else decided to enter the sliding doors.

"She went to look for her certificate, but she hasn't returned yet. I put a call into Vegas to inquire regarding any record of the union there, and they should be getting back to me momentarily."

"She shouldn't get anything, anyhow. If she did marry him, she must have only done it for the money…"

Nancy felt her cheeks burn. How dare this woman insinuate such a thing!

"If she married him, and I think she did, she's entitled to half."

"I don't happen to agree with you, and perhaps you ought to remember which side your bread is buttered on. I'll fight this." Isabelle's high heels clicked away.

Nancy held her breath waiting for John's retreat. Instead, his footsteps drew nearer before coming to a stop dangerously close to her hiding place.

"Why don't you come out now, Ms. Moran? The coast is clear".

CHAPTER 11

▼

With her cheeks still flushed and burning, Nancy stepped out of the foliage. She should have realized that with the bright light behind her, she was far easier to see through the leaves than they were in the dim interior "It-it really isn't the way it looks," she began.

"I'm sure it isn't," John said solemnly and waited, his arms folded across his chest.

"I-I couldn't see. I couldn't see and so I stopped."

"But you could hear?"

"Well yes, I heard, but-but then it was too late."

"Then you must have heard me say that I was confident that your marriage to Greg Moran will soon be verified."

Before Nancy could answer, Claudia came running in slamming the screen and pushing the plants aside. Gone was her tennis racket and her bow tied pig-tails. Now her braids encircled her head giving her a more mature look, and she carried a book in one hand instead of a racket. When she saw the two of them standing in her way, she stopped for a moment, then reached over and plucked a dead leaf from Nancy's golden mane. "You and the barrister been in the bushes?" she asked impudently.

The sound of a telephone ringing down the hall saved them from having to respond.

"I think that's probably for me," John said, escaping quickly toward the library.

Claudia still gazed at Nancy mischievously. "Your cheeks sure are pink," she said. "And you're breathing awfully fast."

Nancy resisted the impulse to smack her. Instead, she said sweetly, "Bet your mother would be interested in knowing her daughter's taste in literature."

Claudia glanced down at the book in her hand. The War and Peace cover was askew so that one could plainly see Lady Chatterly's Lover peeping out beneath it. Undaunted, she burst out laughing. "So we're even." she said. "I won't tell if you won't." And she tore up the stairs still laughing good humoredly.

Nancy shook her head. What a brat. What an adorable brat.

"Nancy, could you join me in the library, please?" It was John.

Silently thanking both Claudia and the telephone for interruptions which had given her time to compose herself before having to face John Stacy again, Nancy walked to the library, head high and chin up. "Yes?" she inquired coolly.

"Your marriage has been confirmed," he said without preamble.

"Yes?" she said again. "And should I be surprised or grateful to learn that what I knew to be true has been confirmed?"

"You must understand. One has to take every precaution in a case like this."

Nancy was glad to see that he was on the defensive now. "Case like what?" she demanded.

"A case involving a large estate. Listen to me. Greg Moran was to receive over a million dollars from a trust fund set up by Amelia Carstairs Moran upon his graduation from college. The interest on that sum alone amounts to a staggering sum. Morania was also to be his."

"But doesn't Morania belong to Isabelle and Ben?"

"No, they have a condo in Louisville, and have had use of Morania (mainly as a summer home) until Greg inherited his trust. Everything had been put in motion for the takeover, when word came of Greg's death. Along with that shock, the family finds out he was married and, well, I guess you can see it's a bit of a muddle." He pushed back his hair. "We'll get it all sorted out though," he said, "and you'll be a rich woman."

"Rich? I don't want to be rich." Nancy looked at him helplessly. "Did-did Greg know? About the money, I mean. Did he know he was getting all that money?"

"Of course he knew. There were papers to sign and decisions to be made. We tried to advise him but-well, to tell you the truth, he didn't seem to take the matter too seriously." He shrugged and pushed at his hair again. "I know this is going to sound stupid, but he rather gave the impression of being bored by the whole thing."

Nancy smiled for the first time. That was the Greg she knew.

"Greg, we've got to talk about money."

"Money is the root of all evil. Didn't you ever hear that, my sweet?"

"But Greg—if we're going to get married, we've got to start saving, and you've got to stop throwing money around so carelessly. I love all the gifts you buy, but sometimes you don't even have gas money."

"Then I stay home. Seems simple to me."

"But Greg, I don't like you to have to stay home."

"So you want me to wear myself to a frazzle. Is that it?"

"Greg, be serious!"

"See—money is the root of all evil. We're quarreling already."

"Greg!"

"Hey, don't worry. I have a fairy godmother to look out for me. She told me if I'd just manage to get out of this worthy institution with some initials after my name, I'd never have to quarrel with my girl about money. She'd also make sure that I always have gas." And he began to laugh. "Burp, burp, burp," he said. "See, it's coming true already."

John Stacy was watching her expectantly. Nancy tried to remember the last thing he'd said, and how she should reply, but her mind was filled with Greg. "Amelia Carstairs Moran," she said. "Greg's godmother by any chance?"

John looked startled. "No—grandmother," he said, "on Ben's side."

"I-I want to think about all this," Nancy said.

"Of course. We'll talk more later."

Feeling as though she'd been put through a shredder, Nancy had difficulty absorbing all that was happening to her. Her thoughts were disjointed, as she tried to concentrate on the changes in her personal status, which had taken place in such a short period of time. She had gone from a financially struggling college girl to a happily married woman to a bereaved widow to an unwelcome daughter-in-law to a rich woman in the space of two shorts weeks. It was just too much to think about, so she forced herself to return to her room and search through her briefcase one more time. She would narrow her focus to one issue only—what had happened to her marriage certificate. Perhaps she could handle that.

Finding her case as devoid of what she searched for as it had been previously, she tossed it aside. Brent had said that she might never have brought it, but she knew that wasn't true. All the way to Kentucky from Nevada she sat stiffly in her seat on the plane, her hand in her briefcase clutching the only tangible evidence left of her marriage. Oh yes, it had been here Then what had happened to it? Had someone taken it? If they had, it was a senseless act. Surely they would realize that it could easily be replaced, that there would be records for verification.

Carefully she took a bit of red ribbon from her pocket. She had found it by the overturned case this morning, but had told no one. Had Shammy dragged it in here from somewhere?

She thought of Claudia with the pigtails tied with red bows, who later appeared with braids in a coronet and no bows. Claudia might steal it just for the lark of it.

She thought of Rosa whose skirt was covered with so many red bows it had been impossible to ascertain if one was missing or not. Rosa might have done it out of jealously or spite. She didn't know her well enough to judge her, but her feelings for Greg certainly appeared to be genuine.

She pulled out her notebook and wrote:

> MARRIAGE CERTIFICATE
> CLAUDIA?
> ROSA?
> PERSON OR PERSONS UNKNOWN?

Written down, it didn't look nearly as serious as it had loomed in her mind. She even smiled at the last entry, person or persons unknown. It was such a bombastic phrase for such a piddling, picayune offense.

Feeling a little better, she decided to try another heading. This time she wrote:

> MONEY

She stared at the word for a long time. Money could do so many things, but from stories she'd done on people who gained wealth suddenly through sweepstakes, she'd found out that it seldom brought happiness. Many of those she'd interviewed had gone back to their old jobs and their old friends after the initial joy had worn off. They needed to feel like productive human beings. She didn't like thinking of herself as a rich woman without effort on her part. It left her even more rudderless than she felt without Greg. How could she lose herself in her work, if she didn't have to work? How could she enjoy the spoils without the struggle? She wanted to get a job and live her life as she'd planned it; only she was going to have to do it without Greg. Under the heading she wrote:

> RETURN IT TO THE MORAN FAMILY

Before putting the notebook away, Rosa's name jumped out at her, jogging her memory. Rosa wanted to talk to her. To avoid another trip downstairs to hunt for her, Nancy stepped out on the balcony. The lawn spread out below her giving the appearance of a green velvet carpet. From this distance one could not see the stray weed or thorn. Is this what distance does? Nancy wondered. Does it cover up life's imperfections? Sometime in the future, would life look good to her again? Would the ugliness of Greg's death fade in the distance, and the bleakness of life recede? She supposed it would, but just like the thorn, in reality the scar would still be there.

At the umbrella table, she saw Rosa's dark head bent close to Brent's blond one. "Come on up, Rosa," she called.

CHAPTER 12

▼

A gentle tap on the door announced Rosa's arrival. Nancy took one look at the gorgeous girl standing there and said, "You sure don't need distance to make you look perfect."

Rosa looked puzzled, but shrugged and smiled. "Thanks," she said. She began pacing slowly around the room picking up items from the dresser and the stand and rolling them between her hands before replacing them.

"What is it you wanted to talk to me about?" Nancy prompted from her seat on the bed.

Rosa's eyes darted to the left and to the right. An image of the Felix cat clock Nancy had as a child, whose eyeballs rotated sideward back and forth with each tick of the clock came unbidden to Nancy's mind. Rosa's pacing became more erratic. She had grabbed the belt from Greg's old robe, and was twisting it between her fingers. Suddenly, she stopped, looked at the belt, then held it up against her cheek. "Greg did give me the ring," she said defiantly, "He did."

"I'm sure he did," Nancy said soothingly.

"And he was going to marry me. I know he was." She grabbed Greg's robe from the bed and slid to the floor with it, breaking into wild sobs.

Nancy, whose own grief was never far from the surface, knelt down, put her arms around Rosa, and cried right along with her. She felt a kinship with this desolate waif, a bond between two people who shared the same pain, the same sense of terrible loss. As their sobbing eventually receded, Nancy's reporter's mind returned and she asked gently, "Did he say that? Did he say he was going to marry you?"

"Not exactly, but that's what he meant."

"What did he say? What did he say exactly?"

"It was after my prom. He was going back to school and I was crying. I told him I loved him, that I wanted him to take me with him. He laughed and said, "Rosie Posie, you always think you're in love. You'll break a hundred hearts before you're through and you won't even remember the crush you once had on older brother type Greg." I kept crying and hanging on to him. He picked up the ring his grandmother had given him. Claudia and I were always trying it on and teasing him to let us wear it. Well, he took the ring and said, "Here, Rosa, you take the ring. You're the only girl I know that could outsparkle this sparkler, anyhow." And he pushed the ring into my hands and me out the door, and that's the last time I even saw him. We all knew his grandmother had given him the ring to give to the girl he was going to marry." Rosa broke into fresh sobs.

Nancy saw the picture clearly. It was so like Greg. Confronted with a crying child, he would think the thing to do was distract it—give it a piece of candy, a trinket and send it happily on its way. Only the child was not a child. It was Rosa. And the trinket was not a trinket. It was a valuable diamond. Oh Greg, she thought. What a dumb thing to do.

"He did love me, didn't he?" Rosa's beautiful swollen face looked up pitifully at Nancy.

"I'm sure he did," Nancy said firmly, "and you have the ring to keep always as a reminder of how special Greg thought you were."

"That's right. I do." The wildness was gone from Rosa's eyes and so was the erratic movement. It was easy to think of her as a child, for with the passing of the storm, she was so quickly sunny again. She paused at the door seeming to search for words. "I'm sure he liked you a lot, too," she said finally, and was gone out the door.

Nancy stared at the closed door, a grin spreading across her face. Any jealousy she felt for Rosa was gone. She was very glad they had a chance to talk.

She tidied her room, then left it to look for Mr. Moran. She wanted to talk to him about his mother and the money.

Mr. and Mrs. Moran remained an enigma to her. Each seemed to live a life entirely independent of the other like two tangential circles, occasionally touching, but then arcing off to travel alone once more. Isabelle's relationship with Ben was hard to determine for the two of them were so seldom together, and when they were it reminded Nancy of tiny children at parallel play. You put them in the same room and they play with their toys side by side but without interaction, each one absorbed in their own world.

She did notice some kind of a relationship between Mrs. Moran and Steve Whitelaw. Mrs. Moran didn't act flirtatious when he was around. She merely acted different. They sought each other's eyes when they were in a room together and it seemed as though those eyes were telegraphing signals or messages. Sometimes they appeared worried or distressed, at other times, relieved. Nancy's inquisitive nature would have liked to have known more, but her sixth sense told her that though something was obviously brewing between the two, it seemed more like a conspiracy than an affair.

Ben, on the other hand, was oblivious to signals or subtleties of any kind. He reacted only to direct stimuli. He preferred engines to people, and spent most of his time at Morania in the boathouse or on the river. He was continually puttering around or tinkering with one piece of equipment or another, dressed in old rumpled clothes with a baseball cap on his head and a greasy rag hanging out of his back pocket. He looked more like some struggling mechanic than the successful Louisville engineer he was supposed to be.

Nancy spied him bent over one of the boats, for she'd been working her way towards the river as she thought about the two Morans. She called out to him though she was still at quite a distance, and could tell by the way he jumped that she'd startled him.

"Hello," he called back. "Are you making another get-away? Take this rowboat here. No one will ever suspect you'd try to get away in it."

"No" she laughed. "Not this time. I've come to chat."

"Well, sit right down," he said taking his rag and dusting off another overturned pail.

"Tell me about your mother," she said.

"My mother?" Nancy saw him stiffen and his eyes grew steely.

"Amelia Carstairs Moran," Nancy urged.

"I know the name," he said in a cold dispassionate manner. "I think I'm the last person you should be asking about her.

"But she was your mother, wasn't she?"

"She was that, but if she could have changed it, she would have."

Nancy remained silent.

"Amelia had no use for those that used their hands, for those that knew how to work for a living. She seemed to forget how the old man started out. He was a worker, that one. But she was a Carstairs. The Carstairs were soft- an old well-known family, but soft. They patronized the arts, dabbled in painting, drama and literature, and had enough people who believed they were creative and talented to keep their name in the public eye and to keep them rich, which was lucky since I think they would have starved if they had to find a real job. They could charm the birds from the trees, the Carstairs, but they were soft." He removed his cap and then squashed it back down on his head. "It was her fault Greg was the way he was. It was her genes and no matter how I tried to toughen him up, he remained soft. He had that charming devil-may-care attitude, was a sucker for every bleeding heart, and was so-so sensitive." He said the last word as if it was a disease.

Nancy stared at him in disbelief. He must be the victim of some deep-seated emotional problems, but she wasn't going to listen to him talk about Greg that way even if he was his father. "I feel sorry for you, Mr. Moran," she said. "It must be awful to carry all that hatred around inside you, but Greg was not soft, unless being feeling and caring makes someone soft. He always stood up for what he believed in, and never allowed anyone to pick on those who couldn't defend themselves when he was around."

"As I said, a sucker for every bleeding heart."

Nancy looked at the closed unfeeling face, and felt herself growing angry. "Greg was kind and good," she said her voice becoming shaky. "Oh I do feel sorry for you. You never got to know your own son, and now it's too late." She left so abruptly she tipped over her pail, but not before she saw something glistening slide down Mr. Moran's leathery cheek and fall off his chin. For a second she wavered. Probably just perspiration, she thought heartlessly and continued back towards the house.

CHAPTER 13

▼

The indignation against Mr. Moran set a brisk pace for Nancy back from the river. Her mind and her feet were synchronized so that the more thoughts that tumbled through her brain, the faster her legs and feet went. Plunging along as she was, she almost trampled poor Melinda, who was lying on her stomach reading a novel by the bushes near the path. Nancy's right foot caught in the blanket Melinda was lying on, and she went sprawling headlong down beside the startled girl. Embarrassed, she lifted her head and said, "Hi."

Melinda smiled shyly. "Nice of you to drop in," she said.

Nancy rubbed her elbows and grinned. "I would have called first, but I didn't want you to fuss."

Now, Melinda was grinning too. "You've caught me at a rather bad time, my dear. I haven't vacuumed my blanket in days." She flicked a finger at a dead leaf. "Let's look you over," she continued. "Did you hurt yourself?"

"Mostly my pride, I think," Nancy said, "though I fear I've dug up my elbows a bit."

"That's what comes of rubbing elbows with us elite bush dwellers," Melinda said. "C'mon, let's go see what Aunt Isabelle has to clean you up with." She helped Nancy up, then picked up her blanket and book.

"That's not Lady Chatterly's Lover, by any chance, is it?" Nancy asked pointing at the book.

"No. Why?"

Nancy told her about Claudia's large War and Peace cover over the much smaller volume concealed inside, and Melinda laughed.

Nancy was surprised at what a pleasant companion Greg's cousin turned out to be. It must have been her shyness that made her seem so dull before. "Guess you can't always judge a book by it's cover," Nancy said, and they both laughed again thinking of the impish Claudia, but Nancy was also thinking of the quiet Melinda.

After patching up Nancy's elbows, the two sat on the edge of a large green bathtub and chatted.

"Amelia Carstairs Moran. She'd be your grandmother, too?"

Mindy nodded.

"Tell me about her. What was she like when you were growing up?"

"She was the most marvelous grandmother in the whole world. Not like anyone else's grandmother, just special in every way. Of course, Greg was her favorite," she said with no detectable rancor, "but she spoiled us all outrageously."

"Is that why she left all her money to Greg? Because he was her favorite?"

Melinda looked startled. "Grannyam wouldn't do that," she said reprovingly." She had trust funds for all of us. Greg's was larger because he was the oldest, and I think she wanted to compensate because Uncle Ben was so hard on him, but she looked after everyone."

"I-I didn't know." Nancy felt she had been gently chastised. "She sounds like a wonderful woman. I wish I'd met her before she died."

"Died! Grannyam isn't dead. She's very much alive. In fact, I'm going over to visit her this afternoon and ride Champion. He's my horse. Grannyam keeps him for me."

"But-but I thought-well how come she left the money, then?"

That was Grandpa's money. She had her own Carstairs's money, more than enough to live very well on. Said she didn't need Grandpa's, and it was too much for one woman to have. So, she divided it up between my mother, Dorothy, and Greg and Claudia's dad, Uncle Ben, and between the three of us, only ours were in trusts to be given to us after we completed college. She feels a college education is very important. Uncle Ben refused to go when he was young. He felt it was for sissies. He eventually got a degree through night school, but he felt it was a waste of time. My mom says he's always been a rebel."

Nancy thought back to the day of the funeral. She knew she'd been very upset, but she thought she'd have remembered meeting Greg's grandmother. "Was she here?" she asked. "The day of the funeral, was she here?"

"She was at the funeral, of course, but she didn't come back here. She was devastated by Greg's death, and well, Uncle Ben quarrels with her a lot. Not that Grannyam ever says a bad word against him, or lets anyone else," she added quickly. "Still, though she only lives a short distance from here, they don't really visit back and forth. I can't believe you thought she'd died. The only dying Grannyam has done is dying to meet you. If I call her so she can fuss and vacuum her blankets, would you like to ride over with me?"

"Of course," Nancy replied at once.

It was only a short time later that the two of them set out, Melinda in jodhpurs and Nancy in a neat tan shirt and skirt that made her hair look more like honey than sunlight.

During the short drive, Nancy learned that Mindy had completed her junior year at the University of Virginia in Charlottesville where she was majoring in nursing. No wonder she'd patched up Nancy so well. A few shy questions and comments and a few expressions that flitted across Mindy's face left Nancy wondering if Mindy had a crush on Brent. Remembering Brent's interest in Rosa this morning, she decided not to try to find out.

When they pulled into a circular drive in front of a huge mansion, Mindy said drolly, "Granny's cottage-humble but cozy." The two went up to the gigantic double doors giggling together as Mindy rang the bell.

The woman who answered the door didn't look like anyone's grandmother. She was slim and trim, dressed in a plum colored pantsuit that exactly matched her lipstick and the paint on her perfect oval fingernails. Slingback heels with open toes showed off the same plum colored polish on toenails encased in nylon coverings. It was the face that impressed Nancy most of all, however. 'Neath short dark frosted hair was a feminine version of Greg's face. It was beautiful. She saw both Greg's and Claudia's dark sparkling eyes, Greg's long narrow face, the same dimples and cleft in the chin. All Nancy could do was stare.

Amelia Carstairs Moran seemed not to notice. She gave Mindy a big hug and kiss, told her how glad she was to see her, then turned her attention to Nancy. "You have to be Nancy," she said, "for you're exactly the way Greg described his new bride." Nancy continued to stare.

CHAPTER 14

▼

"You-you knew about me?" Nancy finally stammered.

"I sure did. There wasn't much Greg didn't tell his Grannyam."

"But the Morans-they didn't know."

"I said there wasn't much he didn't tell his grandmother. There were things he didn't share with his parents." She smiled conspiratorially at Nancy, and pulled the two girls inside. A tall distinguished looking man stood in the hall, disapproval showing on his face. "Now Bronson," she addressed him, "there's no need for you to look at me like that. The day a grandmother can't open her own door for her own granddaughter is a sorry day indeed. He thinks it's not my place to open the door," she told the girls as if he wasn't there.

Bronson's mask of disapproval slipped as affection took over, "Excuse me. Ma'am," he murmured. "Please ring if you need me." He gracefully withdrew.

"Poor Bronson. He tries so hard to protect me and I'm such a trial to him."

"Oh, Grannyam, you're a trial to everyone, demanding your own way all the time, and doing it in such a manner that everyone forgives you immediately. Don't go playing the innocent with Nancy."

Amelia chuckled. "Mindy, you minx. I think you understand your grandmother a little too well." She led them into a room with an ornate carved fireplace. A teacart set for three was pulled up in front of it. "Let's have our tea," she said, "and then Mindy can slip off and visit Champion, and Nancy and I can have a long talk."

Amelia poured the tea, and they sipped daintily from their fragile china cups, as they munched on tiny cakes and engaged in polite conversation. The affection between Melinda and her grandmother was obvious, but Nancy did not feel left out. Amelia asked about everyone at Morania. She was amused by Claudia's antics as relayed by Mindy, and interested in everyone's activities. Nancy was contented to merely be there. She felt part of this woman's family, as she never had with the Morans. She could see Greg in every expression, in every gesture, in the very being of his grandmother, and while painful, it pleased Nancy. As long as there was an Amelia, a part of Greg lived on.

"I know you're anxious to see Champion, Darling, and Bronson, who gets his information from the groom, says Champion has been missing you, too. So run along to the stables and have a nice ride. The two of us will have a cozy chat." She hugged and kissed Melinda, who ran off eagerly to greet her beloved horse.

Amelia rang a bell, and Bronson immediately appeared to trundle away the remains of their tea. "Now tell me about Greg," Amelia said, settling herself back in her blue velvet wingback chair. "Tell me everything."

And Nancy did just that. She relived every glorious moment and every second of pain and desolation, and through it all Amelia sat erect in her chair listening attentively, her expressive face mirroring her feelings, but always in control. Only her plum colored nails betrayed the depths of her suffering. Nancy watched their rounded tips dig into the blue velvet fabric, through the telling of her story, and when she had finished, mentally and emotionally drained, she watched, fascinated, as the dents made by those nails slowly filled in. Would that the void in Amelia's and her lives could be so easily filled, she thought.

"Please tell me what Greg told you about me," Nancy pleaded after a pause.

"He told me you were a great looking chick, which you are, level headed, which you seem, and the only girl he'd ever marry, which he did. He also said he was crazy about you on page after page and in every way imaginable. You were fun; you were funny; you were smart, modest, lovable, kind, good with money, but generous. You were everything he ever wanted." She panted for breath. "And that was one of his shorter notes." She smiled. "One day, when I feel more up to it, I'll go through his letters and let you read them for yourself. There was no doubt that he loved you, my dear."

Tears began to well up in Nancy's eyes. Amelia squeezed her hand and changed the subject.

"Have you met Rosa?"

Nancy nodded.

"What do you think of her?"

"She's very beautiful," Nancy had herself under control at last, "and I think I like her."

Amelia looked rather surprised, but there was no time to pursue the subject for Melinda was back.

"Hi, you two," she said in her quiet manner.

"How was your ride, darling?"

"Great. Champion was a bit headstrong. He pranced around and was determined to pass by the front drive. I think he knew there was someone new here, and he wanted to show off. When I wouldn't let him, he pawed and pouted for a while, then flicked his tail and pretended he could care less. I noticed him casting an eye in this direction whenever he thought I wasn't looking though."

Amelia chuckled. "I swear you think that horse is human, Mindy, and, of course, the groom, Corey agrees with you."

"Well, Corey was casting his eyes in this direction, too, so I couldn't get his attention to ask." Melinda giggled.

"Isn't she great?" Amelia asked Nancy.

"She is that. I'm very glad I got to know her better." Nancy remembered how dull and mousy she imagined Mindy at first.

Melinda looked straight into Nancy's eyes reading her thoughts exactly. "Can't always judge a book by its cover," she said with a twinkle in her eyes.

Amelia paid no attention to this interchange. "I was truly blessed when it comes to grandchildren; three-" Her voice faltered for a minute and Nancy knew she was thinking of the one she'd lost, but she quickly continued, "three beautiful individuals, each one so totally different from the other two, but each precious in his own right, just like my two children were. I have been truly blessed." She bowed her head for a minute, then lifted it clear eyed. "And you, my dear Nancy, make grandchild number four."

Nancy could hardly breathe. For the first time she was a part of Greg's family.

"Grannyam, this precious grandchild is going to take Number Four, and leave before you find out that we may be what is known as a mixed blessing."

Amelia laughed and hugged them both. "I'm so glad you came," she said. "Please come back soon."

Bronson appeared as if by magic to open the door. After one more hug, the girls ran down the steps to the car with Amelia stepping out on the porch to wave to them. As she was about to get in the car, Nancy turned suddenly. "I forgot something," she said, and bounded back up the stairs. "About the money," she said softly to Amelia, "I don't intend to keep it."

Amelia smiled and gave her a gentle pat. "You may change your mind once you read those letters," she said cryptically.

CHAPTER 15

▼

"Let's not go back yet, Mindy. Let's catch a bite somewhere." Nancy was reluctant to return to Morania.

Melinda glanced at her clothing. "I'm not really dressed for the Seelbach, but I'd like to take you there."

"What's the Seelbach?"

"It's an old hotel that's been recently restored." She glanced at her watch. "It's early enough that we could eat in the less expensive dining area or coffee shop. I forget what they call it. Oh, but I'm so horsy," she moaned. She thought for a minute, then neatly altered their course. "I know what I'll do," she said smugly.

A short time later, they were in a glassed in concourse containing a shopping mall. Melinda left Nancy in Walden Books. "A journalist should be happy here for a short time," she said. "I have an errand. Be right back."

Nancy wandered around contentedly until Mindy returned wearing a new plain navy skirt and blouse, and carrying a large plastic bag. Nancy pointed at it, "The jodhpurs?" she asked.

Mindy grinned and nodded. "It wasn't easy removing Champion's distinctive odor in a small washroom," she said, "but I tried. The remains of it will help you locate me, should we get separated, however."

Nancy followed her out of their glass mall into a closed off street lined with tiny shops. It looked so interesting, Nancy would have liked to explore it, but they stopped almost immediately before a distinctive building with a tall tophatted Abe Lincoln like doorman, who didn't seem to mind their casual attire in the least.

They entered another era in the refurbished Seelbach, which they toured a bit before eating and talking, talking, talking. Mindy told Nancy how she'd always wanted to be a nurse, how she'd suffered through microbiology, anatomy, physiology, chemistry, pharmacology, etc., and she felt she was never going to make it. In her junior year she'd started her clinical rotation, and, at last, felt like a nurse. She described the patients she'd cared for, the good feelings she had when she knew she'd helped someone. She discussed the thrill of watching a delivery in obstetrics, and talked about the children in peds, and the elderly in the geriatric wards. Whether discussing the young or the old, her face glowed as the words flowed.

Nobody could think this girl mousy or dull if they saw her now, thought Nancy, as they finished up with a piece of a sweet concoction called Seelbach pie. "If I keep eating like this, I'm going to need a nurse." Nancy pushed at the remainder of her pie with her fork.

"Don't look at me," Mindy giggled. "I haven't learned the treatment for 'stuffed toads', yet. At the moment I sure am able to empathize with the signs and symptoms, however. Let's get out of here while we can still fit through the door."

The ride home was quiet. Nancy was too full to talk much and guessed Mindy was the same. Back at Morania, they entered a house that seemed deserted, but voices from the dining area told them it was only because everyone was at dinner. "Let's change into jeans and go for a walk to help burn up some of the calories we've ingested."

Nancy nodded gratified for the low voice Mindy had used, for she didn't feel like facing anyone right now, especially Ben. They raced silently up the stairs.

By the time Nancy had changed into jeans and a dark plaid shirt, washed her face and run a comb through her hair, Mindy, also in jeans with a white cardigan draped around her shoulders, was at her door. The two slipped downstairs and out into the evening air. They headed for the river at a brisk pace. "Walking is really better than jogging," Mindy explained. "It's less damaging to your articulating surfaces."

"Then, thank goodness for my articulating surfaces," Nancy said, puffing along beside her.

A short time later they were at the river's edge. "A poor idea to come this way," Mindy observed. "It certainly limits a walk."

"Why do you think I headed this way?" Nancy smiled. "We journalists are more used to pushing a pen than pushing our muscles. I wanted to preserve myself."

"You weakling," Mindy sneered.

"It was really you I was worrying about, Mindy," Nancy said. "I don't want you to have to do CPR out there on the trail. Besides," she giggled," if my hearing was correct, you were panting almost as much as I was. You hardly had breath for one, let alone two." She stepped into the rowboat. "Here," she said patting the seat beside her. "Sit down. I won't tell anyone, and I'm sure your articulating surfaces will be ever so grateful."

Mindy sniffed and settled down beside Nancy. "I'm only doing this because I don't want your collapse on my conscience," she said.

"Let's row out a little ways," Nancy said. Noting Mindy's reluctance, she added, "Great upper body exercise to complete our rehab program."

Mindy grinned. "I'll shove off," she said, "but we shouldn't go far. It'll be dark before long." After a mighty heave, Mindy scrambled into the boat and sat back down. The current was swift, and they let the boat drift out a ways before they got themselves organized to row.

"Okay," Nancy said as they sat side by side on the middle seat. "Yo-oh, heave ho. Together now." And they dipped their oars into the dark water.

Crack! "Oh Oh, not Yo-oh" Mindy said. "I think I've broken mine." She lifted her oar out of the water, and the two girls stared, for the entire widened end was gone. Mindy looked frightened.

"Never fear," Nancy said. "I mostly push pen, but I also know how to paddle a canoe. You move to the back and I'll use my oar as a paddle." They removed Mindy's broken oar, and took Nancy's from its oarlock. Somehow, she got them turned and headed back toward Morania. Just as they were breathing a sign of relief, there was another sickening crack. Hesitantly, Nancy lifted her oar paddle. The end was hanging at a precarious angle. As she tried to bring it aboard hoping to repair it, it struck the side of the boat, and its injured part disengaged itself and disappeared below the surface of the silent water.

The two girls looked at each other helplessly. At almost the same moment, they both began shouting for help.

The distance Nancy had regained was quickly being lost and Morania began to grow smaller and smaller. Not only that, it was beginning to get dark. Nancy hated to think of what would happen to them without lights if a larger boat should happen by. Look Mindy," she said, her voice hoarse from shouting. "I think I see someone by the shore at Morania. See that tiny figure. Look. It's waving its arms." The two began screaming and waving their arms. "Take your sweater and wave it," Nancy instructed Melinda. "It will be more visible."

The figure disappeared, and they heard the sound of a motor. "Hooray," Mindy said. "Whoever that was, they're coming to get us."

Nancy watched the boat approaching at full speed. The front end was so far out of the water, she couldn't see the driver. *If I can't see him, how can he see us?* she wondered. Her mind was also filled with worry about those oars though she'd said nothing to Mindy. Reason told her it was no accident when two oars snapped within seconds of each other. The rescuer gunned the motor and bore down on them with no sign of changing course. A terrifying thought struck. "Oh my God," Nancy yelled to Mindy. "They're coming to finish us off." Her words were cut short by her own screams.

CHAPTER 16

▼

"You almost killed us." Nancy was shaking, whether from the cool night air or from fright, she wasn't sure. She was addressing a white-faced John Stacy, who had just helped them from the rowboat he'd finally managed to tow ashore. "You must have been crazy driving like that." She added shakily.

But John Stacy wasn't listening. He was kneeling on the ground, retching and vomiting intermittently. Nancy knelt beside him. He fumbled in his pocket and brought out a neatly folded handkerchief, which he used to dab ineffectually at his face and clothes. "I'll get some water," Nancy said, jumping up and starting for the boathouse. She had no idea if there was running water there or not, but action seemed better than inaction.

"What's going on down there?" Ben Moran came around the end of the boat-house.

"I-I'm looking for water."

"You're going the wrong way. The water's that way." Ben pointed toward the river.

Nancy felt foolish. She'd never thought of the river. "I meant fresh clean water," she said defensively.

Ben pointed to a faucet coming out of the ground by the boathouse, and as she rinsed the handkerchief, he repeated. "What's going on?"

"That boat you kept offering me had faulty oars, which left Mindy and I stranded on the river. Sir Galahad over there decided to save us and almost rammed into us with your motorboat."

Mr. Moran went directly to the rowboat, Nancy following behind, and examined the oar stubs. "These were cut," he said.

Nancy handed the wet cloth to a still pale and sicklooking John, and said, "They looked okay, but of course, we didn't examine them closely."

Mr. Moran ran his fingers over the broken ends. "Smooth," he muttered. "Looks like they were cut with a hacksaw." He held one up close to his face. "And that looks like plastic wood," he said. "It certainly was a darned fool trick someone tried to pull." He threw the stubs to the ground in disgust, and began fussing with the motorboat. He didn't inquire into the welfare of Nancy, Mindy or John. His concern appeared to rest more with his boats than with the people who had used them.

Nancy began shaking again. John noticed, despite his own condition and said, "You girls need to get up to the house. You're really chilled." Melinda, reverting to old habits, had blended silently into the background, but John pulled her forward, and started them marching back to Morania; a sorry looking general with his very small dilapidated army.

Once back at the house, the girls were shepherded upstairs, and John went off with Brent. Nancy hugged Mindy and withdrew gratefully into the haven of her room. She filled her tub with hot steamy water and bubble bath, and immersed her cold tired bones into it. Later, she washed her hair and lathered cold cream on her face, before wrapping Greg's robe around her. "You can help me figure this out", she said drawing her notebook out. Could Mr. Moran have engineered this? If so, it could only be described as a pointless joke. Add to that his natural love for boats, motors and cars, and his constant polishing and repairing of them, and it was hard to imagine he would deliberately destroy any part of them.

It didn't seem that she or Mindy could have been chosen victims, for who could know that they'd use the boat or that it would be at dusk, a far more dangerous time to be on the river in a rowless rowboat? She tried to remember who besides Mr. Moran had been near the boathouse in the morning. She'd seen Brent coming from that way, but he'd quickly denied being near the boat. Later, Rosa had also walked up from that direction, and Melinda had been reading a book by the path. Even though Mindy had been one of the victims, Nancy remembered she had been reluctant to get in the boat. She wrote all the names in the notebook, but she knew she was being ridiculous. Anyone could have been near the river without her knowing it. These were just the people she'd happened to see.

She wondered if the crowd at the Captain's Table might have gotten rowdy. They could have come by boat later at night and done it as a prank. She remembered the hi-jinks the patrons of the Pink Pussycat often indulged in.

And then there was John Stacy. How did he happen to be on the shore at that hour? She'd never seen him there before.

She pushed the notebook aside. She wanted to forget all these problems, get a job and leave Morania-the sooner the better. She'd do something about it tomorrow.

There was a light knock on her door. "I'm busy," she said. She didn't want to talk to anyone tonight. The knocking stopped. She removed the towel she'd wound around her wet head, and walked over to look again in the mirror. "A real frump," she told herself. There was another knock, louder this time. Only Claudia would be so persistent. "Go away, Claudia," she said. "I'll talk to you tomorrow."

A short silence ensued. Then, "It's not Claudia. It's John. I'll only take a minute."

She clutched Greg's robe together in the front, for she couldn't find the belt. With her other hand, she opened the door and stepped out into the hall, partially closing the door behind her to cut down on the light and her own visibility. She didn't want John to see her too clearly.

"I-I was worried about you," John stammered. Nancy was amused. He'd probably never seen a bona fide frump before. "Are you sure you're all right?"

"Yes, I am, and I suppose I should thank you," she said, "but I think I aged twenty years when I saw you coming straight toward us full speed ahead. Whatever possessed you to drive like that?"

"I," There was a long pause. "I never operated a motorboat before," he said sheepishly.

"What? What made you attempt such a thing?"

"I had to save you," he said simply.

"Save us? You almost did us in. I thought we were going to have to swim to shore." She hoped she'd reduced her accusing tone to a lighter approach.

He gave her a weak grin. "At least **you** can swim," he said.

"John Stacy. You mean you got in a motorboat you didn't know how to run, and attempted a water rescue, when you couldn't even swim! That was a dumb, foolhardy," she softened her voice, "brave thing to do." She looked at him for a long moment. "What were you doing there in the first place?" she asked.

"I was looking for you. We were at dinner, and I heard you come in, and then I heard you go out. I needed to see you so as soon as I decently could I excused myself, and went to look for you. I saw a white sweater down toward the river so I followed. By the time I got there you were already out in the boat. I saw you

shouting and waving, so I waved back. When I realized you were in trouble, I"—
He stopped talking and was watching her right cheek in fascination.

Horrified, Nancy could feel a glob of cold cream traveling slowly down her face.

She reached up and tried to brush it away, but John brought out another folded white hankie (Did he have an endless supply?) and gently mopped it up. He put a hand on each of her shoulders. "I'm so glad you're all right," he said. Then his arms were around her and his lips were on hers.

At first she was so shocked, she just stood there, but then, as if of their own volition, both of her arms crept around his neck and she was kissing him back.

"I'm glad my son can't see this." Isabelle Moran stood there glaring at the two of them.

John jumped backward. "This isn't the way it appears, Mrs. Moran," he said formally. "I was simply trying to comfort this young lady after her trying experience."

Mrs. Moran said nothing, but looked the two of them over from top to bottom. Nancy reclutched the gaping robe and hoped there'd been no bareness exposed. Perhaps there hadn't for Mrs. Moran ignored her completely. "I'll see you tomorrow," she told John coldly. "In the meantime, you ought to wash your face." Her high heels tapped away.

Nancy looked at John. Her dripping hair had left wet patches down the front of him, and a small gob of cold cream now slid down his face straight towards his mustache. He didn't seem to notice. "I'll contact you tomorrow, then, Ms. Nancy," he said in the same formal manner. "Goodnight."

"Goodnight," Nancy said in a small voice, and withdrew with as much dignity as she could muster. Once inside, she touched her lips, which felt like they were burning. How could she have let him do that? How could she have responded to him? She loved Greg. But, Greg wasn't here and she was alone. She had needed comforting just as John had said. That must be it. She went to the bathroom and scrubbed her lips till they hurt.

She crawled into bed wrapping Greg's robe around her. No one could ever take his place in her heart. It was only her fickle body that had betrayed her, and then only out of gratitude for John's foolhardy, but brave act on her and Mindy's behalf. Yes, that was it. Before closing her eyes, she realized that she'd never found out what John Stacy had needed to see her about.

CHAPTER 17

▼

Nancy woke the next morning with a new determination to find a job and leave Morania. Even though Mindy and Amelia made her feel less isolated, she wanted to be away from the oppressive atmosphere, the bizarre tricks, if that's what they were, and away from the disturbing presence of John Stacy. She decided the Louisville Courier Journal would be the place to start. It had been well thought of at Rutgers, a paper that had been owned by the Bingham family for years, but had recently been taken over by Gannett. She dug out one of her neat commercially done resumes and a portfolio of clips before heading for the shower.

She chose the same green suit she'd worn to her first meeting with John Stacy, the one that Greg said made her eyes glow like cats' eyes, the perfect outfit for his perfect kitten. She decided to wear low heel practical shoes, in the hopes that she'd look more like a candidate for a job of levelheaded reporter than for a Pink Pussycat hostess.

Downstairs, she met Mrs. Moran, who stared at her accusingly, before handing her a note. Nancy escaped from her sly knowing look before glancing at the note, which was from John, a formal terse note. He had gone in to his office, and had taken the liberty of making a one o'clock appointment for her. She was to call if she was unable to keep it. She was surprised at how empty his lack of warmth made her feel. You're just missing your husband, she chastised herself, and comfort from anyone seems mighty important at the moment. Get a hold of yourself, Girl.

She wandered back upstairs, her determination to get her life in order delayed by the hour, much too early to present herself at the Chronicle's doors so instead she knocked at Melinda's.

Mindy was still in her pajamas, bunny slippers with long blue and white checked ears on her feet. She looked tired, but none the worse for her unexpected voyage the night before. "Hi," she said, looking up from her book. "What's up?"

Nancy mentioned her plans for the day. She thought Mindy might want to go into town with her. "Surely, there's some shopping or something you could do while I go to the Chronicle and visit John's office," she coaxed.

"There is a nursing state board review book, I've been wanting to get," Mindy said slowly.

"Good. That settles it." Nancy was delighted. She didn't want to see John alone today, other than in the business-like confines of his office. Alone, she might be talked into having lunch with him, or going for a walk, or who knew what else. With Mindy along, there would be no chance of that. The previous night had left her more shaken than she cared to admit, she decided.

The door burst open and Claudia's bright face was thrust through the aperture. She was so tiny; it was hard to remember she was nineteen. "Hey Nance, I want to show you something," she said with no preamble.

"What?"

"Never mind. Just come along. Mindy looks like she needs time to get herself together this morning anyhow".

Nancy hesitated, then grinned at Mindy, and followed this mischievous sprite down the hall, and around the corner to the family wing. Stopping in front of the last door, Claudia said, "I think it's time you saw Greg's room." She stepped away. "Go ahead," she said.

All the feelings Nancy had experienced before opening the door to her own room that first day at Morania, returned full force as she stood in the hall, her hand on the doorknob. Shaking herself, she pushed the door open and stepped inside.

Looking around the neat room, she found she had nothing to fear. Greg's room at Morania bore no trace of his personality. It was just a room whose only link with Greg seemed to be the pile of packing cases Brad had shipped from Rutgers, and which now stood in one corner. Gazing around at the simple maple furniture, Nancy saw the reason for Claudia's invitation. Propped on the dresser was a picture of Claudia and Rosa with Greg in the middle, an arm carelessly draped around each girl's shoulder. Rosa's arms were crossed to show off the now familiar diamond. Since Rosa had said, she hadn't seen Greg after she'd gotten it, Nancy had to assume the picture was taken one of those times they'd coaxed to wear it. Nancy had to break off a chuckle at the audacity of the perseverant Claudia, who remained in many ways immature for her age, a typical kid sister. She supposed Greg's death and going away from home for the first time, as she'd be doing in September, would make her grow up fast enough. Still, she meant to confront her.

She found her at the window looking out at the front of Morania.

"Listen you," Nancy began. "I think you enjoy playing the imp, but I think it's an act. Greg said you were very intelligent. Why must you keep playing games? Rosa and I had a long talk, and I know all about that ring."

If Claudia felt ashamed or disappointed, her small face didn't register it. All it showed was excitement. "It's grandmother", she said. "Get Mindy and come down. Grandmother's here." And she bounded away.

Mindy's response to Claudia's news as relayed by Nancy was no less surprising than Claudia's own. "Grandmother? Here? Why, she never comes to Morania." And Mindy began grabbing clothes and discarding them in a frenzy. Eventually an outfit was chosen and donned, but as they descended the stairs, Nancy looked down at Mindy's feet and suppressed a smile, for peeping out from under her trim baby blue slacks were the whiskers of the bunny slippers she still wore.

At the foot of the stairs by the entry hall, Isabel was fluttering about nervously. "Are you sure you won't come in for a while, Amelia?" she asked the unruffled chic woman standing there with an arm about Claudia.

"No thanks," Amelia answered. "I just brought some things over for Nancy," and she indicated the large brown manila envelope she was holding. "I'm on my way to the hairdresser."

Nancy took the proffered envelope with a questioning look, while Mindy snuggled next to her grandmother on her now unencumbered left side. Amelia squeezed each girl in turn looking very ungrandmotherly in her smart bright red suit and matching snakeskin shoes and bag. "The papers I told you about," she reminded Nancy.

Oh, it must be Greg's letters, Nancy thought, and she hugged the envelope to her body.

"And how are you, Ben?" Amelia addressed her son who stood far back from the others leaning against the newel post, arms crossed over his chest, his body language clearly signaling his non-receptiveness.

"I make out okay, Mother," he drawled. "Of course," and he uncrossed his arms and stretched both of them out towards Amelia, "I do get a bit of dirt under my fingernails from time to time. I know how offensive that is to a Carstairs."

"Now Ben," Isabel interjected.

Amelia cut in. "Ben," she said tiredly, disengaging herself from the girls and walking towards him. "You've got something in your head that just isn't true, and nothing I say ever changes it. I guess you come by your stubbornness honestly, from both sides of the family, but you need to take a good honest look at things. I've never tried to dissuade you from doing the type of work you enjoy, and I've never looked down my nose at you. I accept you and admire you for the person you are, just as I accepted and admired Greg for the person he was. Why couldn't you do the same—for him and for me?" She reached out towards him and it looked as though he was going to take her hand.

Instead he held his short stubby hand next to her perfectly manicured one and said, "There's just too big a difference. We can never understand each other."

"There's a difference between understanding and accepting," she murmured, but she stepped away from him, and after hugging and kissing all three girls, she made abrupt good-byes and left in a chauffeur driven limo.

"What did she bring?" Claudia asked curiously.

But Nancy didn't feel like opening the envelope in front of the others, especially with the present tension in the air. Still hugging the brown parcel close to her, she shrugged, "Just some writings of hers that I was interested in." And that really is the truth, she told herself, as she carried her bundle upstairs and deposited it in her valise.

After a last look at herself in the mirror, she gave a yell to Mindy to exchange slippers for shoes, for she was anxious to see about that job.

CHAPTER 18

▼

"We don't ordinarily hire people right out of school. Your best bet would be to work on a small paper for a while, get some experience, then try us again, or go on and get your masters."

"But I have experience," Nancy persisted. "I had two summer internships, and was literary editor of the school paper. Did you look at my clips?" She thrust her portfolio forward, but the editor-in-chief merely nodded.

"Yeah, I looked at them." The big man sitting across from her was a typical newspaperman, a rough, gruff, no nonsense type, but he didn't frighten Nancy. She'd worked hard to prove herself at each paper she'd been at, and she felt she'd paid her dues. After spending an hour writing headlines, typing out stories from the facts he'd given her, and proving she knew how to work the computers and could paginate, she wasn't going to be dismissed so easily.

"Then you know I can write. There's everything here from hard news to features. My reference letters say I'm hard working and dedicated, and that whoever hires me will be lucky. Just what are your objections to me as an employee?" Nancy trained her green eyes at him levelly, and was surprised to see a slight flicker of interest in his own brown ones.

"Internships aren't the same as work experience," he said slowly, but Nancy knew better. She'd turned out more articles than any other intern and worked side by side with the regular staff earning their friendship and respect. She was about to protest when he continued. "But mainly, I don't feel you're tough enough yet. Go into the minors for awhile before tackling the big leagues."

A bit of the temper, seldom seen but ever present, that went with her red gold hair stiffened Nancy's spine. "Although I may be young in your eyes, Mr. Flaherty, I've sustained enough hard knocks to make me tough enough to handle whatever I must. And speaking of the big leagues, this isn't exactly the New York Times, you know." She feared she'd gone too far, but the big man grinned, and ran a hand through his own shock of red hair.

"Truce," he said. "We do have an opening for a reporter on city desk, but I have a slew of applicants, mostly more experienced people. I'll still consider you, but I've been honest about our policy. Your chances are slim."

"Fair enough." Nancy shook hands with him. "That's all I can ask."

Flaherty grinned. "You may not be tough, but you do have spunk," he said. "I'll get back to you in a week or so."

Out on the street again, Nancy made her way to meet Mindy, who was waiting for her on a bench reading a NCLEX Nursing Review Book. By the size of the bag on the bench with her, it wasn't the only book she'd bought. She looked up at Nancy's approach, stretched and yawned. "Well, I guess I'm ready for the nursing boards. The answer to half these questions is to allow the patient to verbalize his feelings. Maybe I could eliminate the rest of my education, and get a job now. How did you make out with yours?"

"Well, I verbalized a few of my feelings, but I'm not sure it was what the doctor, or nurse, ordered in this case." Nancy went on to explain about her interview as the two made their way to a small restaurant Mindy knew of in the area. There they had salads and iced tea for lunch, feeling virtuous after their gluttony of the day before. By the time they'd finished, it was time for Nancy to meet with John.

Nancy walked to a craftshop with Mindy, who was looking for a Precious Moments Nurse cross-stitch to work on. They made arrangements to meet at an outdoor café after Nancy finished at the law office. Then, Nancy took a cab to Stacy and Spinks.

Disembarking from the cab at a plain colonial brick office building, Nancy realized she could have walked, it was so close, but Mindy hadn't been sure of its location. Not much of an investigative reporter, she told herself. She realized that her heart was beating faster and her palms were sweaty. She had noted no such signs of tension at the Chronicle, where she should have been nervous, but, then again, she hadn't allowed herself to get entangled in an embarrassing scene with Mr. Flaherty, as she had with John Stacy. Now, she had to face this man, who, it seemed always brought out the worst in her, and let him know how meaningless the whole affair-no, not affair-how meaningless the whole episode had been. Bracing herself, she entered the building and gave her name to the secretary.

Before she could find a magazine to look at, John was standing beside her. "Come right in," he said holding the door for her to pass into his office. Once seated, he began immediately, again the formal Mr. Stacy, not the John of the hallway scene, which immediately reassured Nancy. She could feel her heart beat slow down and her palms begin to dry up as he began abruptly. "I have some news for you, Ms. Moran, that I'm sure you'll find most surprising."

"Yes?" Nancy prompted. "Is this what you were going to tell me last night?"

He looked shamefaced for a moment and nodded, then resumed his serious demeanor. "It's a completely unexpected development, something we've just learned,"

"Yes?" Nancy again urged.

He held up a long legal sized envelope. "This came in the mail yesterday," he said.

Nancy looked at the envelope. It had a law firm's name in the upper right hand corner, and the return address was New Brunswick, New Jersey. "What is it?" she asked.

John studied her face, for what Nancy couldn't guess, then pulled a document from the envelope. "This", he said dramatically," is the last will and testament of your late husband, Greg Moran."

CHAPTER 19

▼

A will was so untypical of Greg, Nancy thought when she was finally alone in her room at Morania. He was like the cricket gaily fiddling with little thought for the future, a failure that she'd often childed him about………

"So, you think I'm irresponsible? Well, to show you what a responsible fellow I am, I'm going to provide for you royally before leaving for Vegas, where there's the possibility I may lose everything including my bachelorhood." He winked. "Why, with me at the helm, Kitten, you might even get to be the TOP CAT."

"And what are you going to provide? A year's supply of cat chow? My picture on the Purina cat calendar? What?"

"You malign me, my pet. You have no faith. Someday you may find you have a diamond collar around that pretty neck, the world at your feet, and all the other cats in town green with envy, and all because of Responsible Greg Moran."

"Oh Greg, I don't care anything about diamonds, just as long as I have you…."

Well, she didn't have him, but he had provided royally. The will clarified that, for he'd left Nancy everything. And what was she going to do about it? If she hadn't wanted half a fortune, what was she to do with all of it? And Morania. It would be hers, but what in the world would one girl do with it?

She thought over her meeting with John Stacy. She'd been so uptight about seeing him after the fiasco of the night before, but she needn't have worried. He'd been completely businesslike, but instead of finding this overbearing and pomp-ous, as she had in the past, Nancy now saw it as a cover-up for innate shyness and insecurity. Lady Chatterly's Lover certainly wasn't the only book around Mora-nia with the wrong cover.

So many thoughts whirled through Nancy's mind. She felt listless. She lay on her bed fingering the empty loops on Greg's robe, and stroking Shammy. She had been stunned when John produced the will, but had said little.

"You do understand the implications here, Ms. Moran?" he'd questioned anx-iously.

She nodded her head, though whether he meant an understanding of the will's contents or the possible reaction of the older Morans, she wasn't sure. She passed like a zombie from his office, where he'd clasped her hand and assured her he'd see her at Morania that evening; had said little to Mindy on the way home, and Mindy in her understanding way didn't push; and come straight to her room. Now, repeating earlier established behaviors, Nancy stopped petting Shammy and reached for her notebook.

She read through the previous notations one by one, amazed at how silly most of them seemed when viewed from the perspective of new knowledge at her dis-posal, knowledge gained in just a few short days. She wrote a maxim across a page. JUST AS DISTANCE COVERS UP IMPERFECTIONS, KNOWL-EDGE UNCOVERS AND UNRAVELS MISCONCEPTIONS AND MYS-TERIES. Of course, she cautioned herself, knowledge, improperly applied, leads to the wrong conclusions. She checked off the problems solving them by the application of new knowledge.

PROBLEM	SOLUTION
Greg and Rosa	No longer a concern since Rosa's explana-tion revealed the true nature of the rela-tionship.
Marriage unknown to Morans	Totally within Greg's character once it was known that his only real confidante was his grandmother.
Claudia's hints in various directions	Totally within Claudia's character once her natural impishness was assessed.

Scott and Fred's attitude	No longer seemed relevant. Probably part guilt and part immaturity. They'd gone off to visit some classmates and were due back today, before leaving for home.
Ben's strange attitude	Some basic problems between him and his mother, which had been carried on through Greg. Mr. Moran seemed to hate seeing the qualities Amelia admired and he didn't have in Greg. Despite the gulf between Amelia and Ben and the gulf between Ben and Greg, the problems were more due to love than hate. Pain was ever present behind Ben's sharp words and bald statements.
Legalities involving Nancy	This one was easy. Her carefree irresponsible Greg had turned out to be a millionaire.
Loss of marriage certificate	No knowledge as yet.
Owner of red bow	No knowledge.
Who tampered with the oars and why?	No knowledge.

She thought of one new problem. Why, oh why had she kissed John Stacy last night? She refused to dignify it by writing it down. As her cheeks began to burn again at the thought, she wished she could make her mind as blank as the space she'd left on the page. She was ashamed and wanted to forget, but her overwrought mind refused to cooperate.

Suddenly, she thought of the solution—Greg's letters to Amelia. She could read those. She hadn't wanted to look at them before; the mere sight of his handwriting could wipe her out emotionally, but now she felt the need to bring him close no matter how painful. Besides, Amelia had hinted that Greg's letters would be useful in determining what to do about all that money.

So, she got up to retrieve Amelia's packet, but search as she would, just like her marriage certificate, the letters were no longer in her valise.

CHAPTER 20

▼

Nancy was angry. She marched down the stairs, her lips pursed and hands clenched. How could someone steal mementos of Greg, property of his beloved grandmother, steal them right out of the room of his widow? It was deplorable.

She heard soft voices in the vestibule, two figures bending toward each other, lips brushing together lightly. She continued on relentlessly. Isabel Moran and Steve Whitelaw sprang apart quiltily. Ha! Turnabout is fair play, thought Nancy maliciously.

"Oh," Isabel said, obviously flustered, "Steve brought Rosa over earlier, since Fred and Scott returned today and she's planning some kind of get-together. Steve was just about to leave."

Steve looked anguished. If he's going to engage in an extramarital affair, he better toughen up, decided Nancy.

"The package Amelia brought me this morning is missing from my room. Do you know anything about it?" Nancy put the question bluntly.

Isabel's hand fluttered. "No-no," she said, giving a rather piteous look to Mr. Whitelaw, who if anything, appeared even more disturbed before excusing himself and scurrying out the door.

"Are you sure you didn't just mislay it?" Isabel asked, as Nancy gave no sign of budging from her position in the doorway.

"Positive," Nancy said. "This isn't the first time something has disappeared from my room. First my marriage certificate, now this. I'm sure someone invades my privacy frequently, for Shammy is always on a different side of the door from where I left her, and I don't think she can open it by herself. I can bolt myself in, but there's no key to the outside. Perhaps I should have stayed at the Galt House."

Isabel said nothing for a moment. Her plump cheeks had a pasty look which made the dots of blusher on them stand out like clown's makeup, two round red islands floating on a sea of white. Her next move caught Nancy by surprise. "Follow me," she said briskly, and led Nancy to the same study where she'd showed her Greg's postcard. After rummaging through the desk drawer, she produced a key. "Take this," she said, "and keep your door locked at all times. We've never used locks and keys at Morania, but I want you to promise you will." She looked at Nancy earnestly and Nancy nodded dumbly. The red islands on Mrs. Moran's cheeks began to blend in with a more normal skin tone once again. "I'm sure there's a logical explanation. Just what was it that Amelia brought you?"

Nancy hesitated. "Just some things of Greg's," she said vaguely.

Isabel was surprised. "Oh?" she said expectantly, but Nancy didn't elaborate. "Well, they're bound to turn up," Isabel said after a slight pause, then continued. "You're wrong about staying at the Galt House. You belong here. I understand Morania will soon be yours."

"It's a shock," Nancy said slowly. "I don't know what to think or say."

"It will take some adjustment on everybody's part, but it will all work out. I'm afraid I haven't been making it very easy for you, but you have to understand, with so much money involved and with Greg not mentioning he'd married, all kinds of possibilities entered my mind. You can understand that, can't you?" She gave Nancy the kindest smile she'd received from this woman yet, patted her arm and then mentioned that the young people were out by the pool, and John Stacy was in the library, and with that she left the room.

Nancy had again nodded dumbly that she understood, and the funny thing was in a way she did. On the other hand, why had Isabel mellowed so suddenly? Wonder if it was Steve Whitelaw who mellowed her, she thought unkindly. Not particularly wanting to talk to John at the moment, she walked out to the pool, where she found a lively scene.

Brent, Mindy, Claudia, Rosa, Fred, and Scott were all draped on various poolside chaises listening to an excited Rosa. Dark eyes flashing, hands punctuating her sentences, she was making plans for a "gigunda" splash party the following night, since Brent, Scott, and Fred were leaving the morning after.

Mindy scooted over to make room for Nancy on her chaise. "Oh I'm glad you're here," Rosa smiled at Nancy. "We're having a party tomorrow, an outdoor dinner, dance, and splash party here by the pool. It will make us all feel better. We've been so down, and it will be good for you, too. Besides, we have to give these guys a great send-off. We're gonna miss 'em around here." She beamed at the guys.

Three pairs of male eyes stared back at Rosa filled with admiration, perhaps even awe. She's sure got them wrapped around her little finger, Nancy thought. She leaned over to whisper this to Mindy, but she saw Mindy watching Brent with such veiled hurt in her eyes that she stopped herself. John Stacy appeared around the gate at just that moment, so Mindy's attention was diverted.

Rosa ran over and took his arm. "You'll come, too, won't you, John?" She smiled up into his face giving him the full force of her amazing black eyes.

"Who could refuse you anything, Miss Whitelaw?" John asked. "Especially when you look so-so fetching," and his eyes joined the others in admiration of the petite figure in the trim short set. Nancy was flabbergasted. "But tell me, what is it I'm coming to?" John continued.

Rosa babbled happily on about the get-together seemingly oblivious to the amount of attention she was commanding. Nancy did nudge Mindy now and whispered, "We might as well be a couple of frumps." Mindy smiled with her lips, but not with her eyes. When there was a break in the one sided conversation, Nancy said, "By the way, have any of you seen the manila envelope Amelia brought over this morning? It's missing from my room."

No longer was Rosa the center of attention. All eyes were riveted on Nancy. They were not filled with admiration. They all looked totally blank.

CHAPTER 21

▼

"You really think someone took the letters, don't you?" John Stacy was walking down to the river with her after the rather embarrassing scene at the pool. Her question had been so abrupt, it sounded like an accusation. After they all denied any knowledge of the whereabouts of the packet, she had escaped, only to be followed by John.

"Someone had to," Nancy said positively. "They're gone, not mislaid. Just like my marriage certificate is gone. It makes me furious. Yet, why anyone would want them is beyond me."

"If only you'd read them. Perhaps, Mrs. Carstairs Moran, who knows their contents, could shed some light on the subject."

Nancy was thankful that he was treating the matter seriously, not insisting they were simply mislaid, and would turn up. "I suppose I could ask her," she said slowly," but I'd rather not tell her I've lost them until I've at least tried to recover them. I'm sure she'll be very upset to lose that last contact from her grandson. Those letters were precious to her, and I feel terrible that they were given into my safekeeping, and now they're missing."

"I can understand that," John said, "but if we knew what they were about, it might give us a clue as to who would take them."

Nancy nodded. "If I don't get them back in a day or two, I'll ask her," she promised.

The river shone up ahead of them, a silvery ribbon in the gathering twilight. With her eyes on the river and not on the path, Nancy stumbled over a root. John reached out to steady her, then pulled her close as he leaned against a tree. She could feel her heart thumping against his rib cage, and the solid warmth of his body next to hers, so like Greg, but not Greg at all. She stiffened and pulled away. "Forgive me," he said. "I'm such an insensitive beast. It's not that I don't respect you or your grieving for your husband, it's just that when I see you frightened or sad, or upset, I always want to comfort or protect you, and end up giving you one more thing to be upset about." He turned from her and headed back at an imprudent speed in the dim light. Nancy stood listening to him thrash around, her emotions in a jumble, before continuing toward the river.

She was looking towards the boathouse, scanning the dimness for the stocky form of Mr. Moran. Just as her perception of Mindy and John Stacy had changed and was still changing, so was her perception of Greg's dad. Her animosity towards him was being tempered by insight into some of his problems. He reminded her of a rebellious little boy when he faced Amelia this morning, a little boy, who though rebellious, was really seeking approval. Add to this the loss of his son who he professed to disapprove of, and the guilt he must feel, because he gave Greg such a hard time. Then, his wife had some kind of relationship with the man next door, and while Nancy had earlier discounted any thought of an affair there, now she was not so sure. Added all up, he became someone more to be pitied than condemned.

Of all the family at Morania, Nancy felt Ben would be most upset by the loss of the estate, for the boats and boathouse were a large chunk of his life. This was why she wanted to find him tonight, to talk about the will, its ramifications, and to reassure him that she didn't want to oust the family from their summer home. What had Greg said about his dad? She tried to remember......

"Pops and I don't exactly see eye to eye. It's more like a tooth and nail existence, and I end up with foot in mouth." He grinned. "Guess that's why Mindy took anatomy-trying to sort the Moran body parts out."

"Oh, Greg. Can't you ever be serious? What's the problem between you and your dad?

"Serious? Greg Moran? That would spoil my image, especially Pop's image of me. Didn't you know? I'm like the Carstairs, a thinker, a dreamer, a playboy, and besides that I can't dismantle and reassemble an engine in fifteen minutes flat. Well, I suppose I could, but it would never run again." He grinned again. "Hey, why are we wasting this gorgeous night? Let's go arm and arm somewhere we can be face to face and neck. Those body parts are more to my liking."

It was Nancy's turn to grin............

"Why are you wasting a gorgeous night like this down by the river, when you could be in the pool?"

Nancy jumped. She hadn't seen the shadowy figure of Ben Moran approaching, being so deep in thought. "I was thinking about Greg," she said, and then she started to cry.

"There, there," he said almost as embarrassed as she was. He didn't pat her or even touch her, just stood there with such a helpless look on his tan weather-beaten face that Nancy tried to stop. She gulped, she hiccoughed, she drew in her breath, but all to no avail. The tears just kept on coming. Ben stood irresolutely, then rummaged around in his back pocket, finally emerging with a large red bandanna. It seemed so incongruous with the luxury of Morania (though no more so than the usual greasy rag that resided there) that Nancy smiled. The smile, however, did nothing to stem the storm that was raging down her face.

"No one but Amelia wants to talk about him," she sobbed. "Everyone else avoids his name like the plague. If I mention something he said or something he did, they're embarrassed, and end the conversation as quickly as possible. I need to say his name, to remember all we've shared, and to hear his family's and friends' memories. It seems to me if we include these memories in our daily lives, then Greg will never die as long as we're around, but if we suppress them, then they're buried just like Greg is, and then he's truly lost to us forevermore." It was a long speech to be gotten through with all the sniffling and snuffling, but Mr. Moran got the message.

"Talk about him to me," he said.

And she did. She talked about how they met, the places they went, the things they did, and all the qualities that endeared Greg to her. She talked about their hopes, their dreams, and their plans. She talked about the things she hadn't known, and the things he did that aggravated her. It was a strange conversation to have with someone she'd have rated least likely to be an understanding listener. It was a strange conversation anyhow, punctuated as it was with frequent mopping up with the red bandanna, and periods when more tears than words came.

Through it all Mr. Moran made no effort to comfort her. He leaned against a tree smoking a pipe, which Nancy had never seen him do before, listening intently when she talked, and waiting patiently when she didn't. Eventually the words and tears began to dry up, and a silence developed between them, a silence that couldn't be classified as either comfortable or uncomfortable, just a silence.

Mr. Moran broke it. "It was good for me to hear this. I guess I needed to see my son through someone else's eyes. I admit my own views are often stubborn and biased, but so are the views of those that try to change them, so I just don't listen. You're biased, too, but at least you presented the whole picture, both the good and the bad as you saw it, and weren't out to convince me of anything."

"Love doesn't mean you don't see someone's faults," Nancy mused. "You just learn to live with them."

"Ah, but human nature is such that along with loving, we like to try our hand at improving. Hence, we constantly have to point out those faults, and suggest ways of dealing with them more effectively."

"You're saying I would have become a nag if-if our marriage would have lasted?"

"I wasn't speaking of you in particular, but it's just human nature."

"I'm sure we'd have quarreled from time to time, but love is also realizing that the other person is also overlooking a lot of your own faults."

"I guess that's my trouble," Mr. Moran said solemnly. "I've never had any faults so it's hard to understand them in others."

Nancy couldn't believe her ears until she saw the twinkle in his eyes. She smiled then remembered why she wanted to see Ben in the first place. "About Greg's will," she began, "I want you to know that I don't want you to leave all this." She waved a hand in a manner that was supposed to encompass all Morania.

"I think I'm through listening," Mr. Moran said and disappeared into the gloom as quickly as he'd appeared, leaving only the pleasant smell of pipe tobacco lingering in his wake.

CHAPTER 22

▼

Nancy looked around for Mindy, but when she found her, alone with her review book in the library, Mindy was quiet and withdrawn. After trying to pull her out of her doldrums with no success, she gave up and wandered back by the pool. All the rest of the 'young people', as Isabel liked to call them, were there. Rosa was still chattering happily about tomorrow's doings, and Brent and John were a receptive audience. Claudia had gathered her own fan club. Fred and Scott, who had always seemed immature to Nancy, were taking turns throwing her into the pool, much to Claudia's delight.

Nancy felt estranged from everyone, as though she was fifty years older than they, but she managed a smile and a "hi".

"Look," yelled Scott and walked on his hands in the pool.

Not to be outdone, Fred crawled up on the roof of the little cabana, and dove into the pool from there.

Claudia and Rosa clapped their hands, but John said soberly, "I wouldn't do that if I were you. It's decidedly unsafe, and could result in a devastating injury." Nancy studied him, and wondered if he felt fifty years older, too. The rest of them laughed and continued their horseplay, but Nancy noticed that the diving stunt was not repeated.

Isabel and Ben, in one of their rare appearances together other than mealtime, arrived with the Whitelaws. Carrying tinkling glasses of iced tea, they moved chairs back from the splashing pool. "There's more tea in the kitchen, a pitcher full. I couldn't carry it," Isabel explained. "I planned to send Claudia for it."

"I'll go get it," said Brent, "since Claudia is swimming."

"I'll go with you," Rosa said immediately.

The two vanished into the house, a very attractive duo, one so dark and petite, the other so tall, lean and blonde. Nancy hoped they wouldn't go near the library, where Mindy was.

The seating arrangement was awkward with Rosa and Brent gone for she and John were too far apart to converse, and the Whitelaws and Morans were separated even further from them both. Nancy felt much as one does when eating alone at a restaurant, at a loss as to where she should look. She watched the three frolicking in the pool, occasionally glancing toward the gate leading to the house, letting her eyes slide casually over the foursome. Ruth Whitelaw had on a white tennis outfit, and though she wore a permanently discontented expression, it was easy to see where Rosa had gotten her looks. Isabel, in pink slacks and a long white top that concealed her figure imperfections, and with her hair in tendrils around her face, looked more attractive then usual. Both of the men were absorbed in their own thoughts. Steve Whitelaw, in tennis shorts like his wife, slumped in his chair and contributed little in the way of conversation. Ben responded to the women if addressed, but seemed fidgety and ill at ease. He had changed his clothes since leaving Nancy earlier, and she wondered if there was a red bandanna in the pocket of his neat gray slacks.

A sudden movement near the cabana distracted her thoughts. She saw a flash of yellow disappear into the building, which she might have dismissed as a product of her imagination, if a spiky yellow tail hadn't wavered outside for a moment longer. She grinned before noticing John was watching her. "It's Shammy," she called over to him, before getting up to see what Shammy was doing.

At first she couldn't see the cat after entering the small building even though she turned on the lights. A scrabbling sound directed her attention to a row of open cubicles, storage areas for those using the cabana. Shammy was in the bottom cubicle, pushing the contents with his paws, as if making a nest to take a nap. She had overturned a talcum container, and the powder was spilled in the cubicle and on the floor. She turned to peer at Nancy, a piece of terrycloth, which Nancy recognized as part of Rosa's hooded robe, draped over her head, and some remnants of white talcum on her little pink nose. Nancy chuckled, but Shammy, unaware or indifferent to her ridiculous appearance, maintained her usual dignity, and strolled over to rub against Nancy's legs, depositing bits of talcum on her navy blue slacks. Nancy reached down and picked up the little cat.

"That's a fine feline you have there." John had apparently followed her again.

"Couldn't you just say 'cute cat'?" Nancy asked bluntly as she stepped out the door.

"It's that, too," John said with a grin, which removed the animosity Nancy had once again felt building between them."

"I guess I'll take her back to the house. I know she wouldn't like it by the pool. Cats don't like water and I think she wants to be near me. Well-uh she does appear inordinately fond of me," she finished feeling slightly foolish at her need to explain.

"Then it has good taste as well as being a cute cat," John said gallantly. "But couldn't you have said, 'she seems to like me'? "he asked mischievously.

"She does that, too," Nancy said laughing at his turnabout.

"Mind if I join you or is three a crowd?"

"No, it's okay. Actually, it will be four, because I was going to join Mindy in the library."

But, they didn't join Mindy in the library, for they met Brent, Rosa, and Mindy; Brent in the middle with one arm draped around each girl, while Mindy carried the iced tea pitcher, and Rosa, the glasses. Nancy was glad to see Mindy smiling and happy, but declined her invitation to come back to the pool, then wished she hadn't for she felt uncomfortable with John. She didn't want to be alone with him again. "I think I'll just go up to my room," she told him.

"I'll walk up with you," he said. Sensing her reluctance or remembering last night's venture in the hall, he added, "I want to talk business a minute."

"Oh?" she said realizing he was following her up the stairs.

"I know you haven't had much time to digest all this, but have you given any thought to Morania? Will you continue to live here?"

"No. No. I'm sure I won't, but I haven't talked to the Morans yet." She didn't mention that she'd tried to talk to Mr. Moran.

"The Morans have known Greg would be getting Morania for a long time. I imagine they're much more prepared than you are to face this."

Nancy wasn't so sure. "They didn't know about me," she pointed out.

"But they may have already been making alternate plans. I don't think you should carry all this guilt around with you. You've had no control over any of the events leading up to this."

Nancy had never thought about it in just this way, but she was feeling guilty, guilty being married to Greg without the Moran's knowledge, guilty about spoiling Rosa's girlish dreams even if they were all illusions, guilty about adding to Isabel's and Ben's unhappiness, guilty about inheriting Moran money, but most of all guilty for being the person to whom their summer home now belonged. And it was also true that she had no control over these happenings; in fact, since coming to Morania she felt totally out of control, pulled deeper and deeper into the lives of those at Morania with the unfolding of each new dramatic event, as if she were being led into a quicksand from which there was no escape. She had to shake off this guilt, and take charge once again of her own destiny.

She reached into her pocket for the key for they had now reached her room. "Thank you, John," she said softly fitting the key into the lock.

"For what?" he asked surprised.

"For being my friend," she said smiling into his handsome face, and trying not to think of the one guilt she'd been blocking from her thoughts all day, the guilt she felt for seeking comfort in the arms of a man who wasn't Greg.

She pushed the door open and said goodnight, but John looked puzzled. "What's that?" he asked pointing to a piece of cardboard that must have been slipped under the door.

She bent down and turned it over. BEWARE. MORANIA WILL NEVER BE YOURS, it said in pasted on vinyl letters.

CHAPTER 23

▼

Nancy slept in the next morning, for she'd been forced to take another sleeping pill the night before. Up until now, she'd felt uneasy at Morania, sometimes aware of unpleasant undercurrents, and sometimes sure someone was playing unpleasant tricks on her, but the crude warning on the cardboard was the first direct indication she'd had that someone wished her ill. Her hands had trembled as she thrust it at John and said, "Take it away. I don't want to look at it."

"I'll take care of it. Don't worry," John said, and giving her an awkward pat had hastened away.

'Don't worry' was useless advice, for once she'd prepared for bed, and slid on Greg's robe, all hope of sleep evaded her. She lay down with eyes wide open wondering who in the world had left such an ugly message. It must be Ben, Claudia, or Isabel since they were the only inhabitants of Morania. Isabel had mentioned that Morania was to be Nancy's perfectly calmly this morning, although she had certainly been against Nancy inheriting anything earlier. What were her true feelings? Nancy was unsure.

Ben? He didn't want to talk about it at all. What did that mean? He had so many hang-ups and could be so cold, she supposed he was capable of it, but she had begun to like him, and somehow felt that he liked her, too. Besides, she was sure he'd use a more direct method of registering displeasure.

Claudia? Claudia was a scamp, and enjoyed putting Nancy in uncomfortable positions, then watching the repercussions, but out and out cruelty didn't seem her forte. Still, she had been cruel the day of the funeral.

Which one? Or could it have been someone acting on the Moran's behalf? Steve Whitelaw on behalf of Isabel? She couldn't picture him creeping up the stairs to shove a handmade sign under her door. She couldn't picture him kissing Isabel either, but he had.

Mindy to avenge her aunt and uncle? Nancy wouldn't believe it. She was her friend. She had been alone in the house for a long time though before Nancy found the sign.

Another ugly thought popped into her mind. What about John? He could be working on behalf of his clients, the Morans. She had never heard of a lawyer, even a friend, who spent as much tome socializing at a client's house as John did. Could it be John? That would be the ultimate betrayal.

She wrote the six names in the notebook. She supposed if she had to choose one name from the list, it would be Claudia. If the young girl was the perpetrator, it reduced the art from sinister to bad taste. She rather hoped it was Claudia.

She thought of each of the six persons, but her mind was no clearer. She thought of Brent, Scott, and Fred, Ruth and Rosa Whitelaw, but could think of no motives for any of them.

'Don't worry' John had said, but worry she did, her mind traveling in dizzying circles until she finally took one of the remaining sleeping pills.

This morning her head felt fuzzy, but a shower helped clear it. She donned some hot pink slacks, and a pink and white striped tee shirt, slipped on some sandals, and felt better able to meet the day.

A knock on her door indicated that Mindy and Claudia were already prepared to meet today and anxious for her to join them. As she let them in Shammy quickly vanished through the open door.

"Rosa's already here preparing for the farewell get-together tonight," Claudia announced. "It's going to be great."

"Do you have a suit?" Mindy chimed in. "You haven't been swimming since you've been here."

A pool party seemed incongruous with Greg's death, but Nancy didn't want to extinguish the excitement the two girls were exhibiting. Besides, Greg would be the first to applaud the idea. "I never unpacked it but I have one somewhere here," she said.

"Find it. Find it." Claudia demanded hopping about. "Is it a bikini?"

"Not a bikini, but revealing enough," Nancy smiled.

"Find it," Claudia again demanded, so Nancy began searching methodically through her unpacked luggage until she pulled out her jade colored Jantzen. Although it was one piece, it crisscrossed over breasts leaving a wide expanse of abdomen provocatively open, and dipped very low in the back, while the leg openings were high cut to reveal her smooth long legs to advantage............

"Wow," Greg said the first time he saw her in it. "A sea nymph and all mine." He regarded her admiringly, as she climbed the steps to the diving board, and dove flawlessly into the pool. Later, when she stretched her lithe form next to his muscular one to 'catch some rays', he admired the suit again. "Bet that makes some interesting tan lines," he grinned.

Still later, on their first night in Vegas as they tumbled into the king-sized bed at the Hacienda, he looked at her critically in her bikini P. Js. "Lucky for you that sea nymph suit left this neat geometric pattern on your abdomen, or I probably would never have found your body so interesting." She threw a pillow at him..............

"Why are you hugging your swimsuit and staring off into space?" Mindy asked gently.

"Sorry. There are so many things to think about. I guess you both know that Greg left everything to me in a will, everything including Morania."

If she hoped to surprise a reaction, she was disappointed. Both girls just nodded and looked at her expectantly.

"Well, how do you feel about it?" Nancy continued.

"I haven't thought much about it," Mindy finally said slowly, "but what was to be Greg's should be yours. Have you made any specific plans?"

"Yeah, are you going to evict us?" Claudia asked impudently. "Not that it might not be a good thing. Summers are usually so boring here, with no young people except Rosa around, and occasionally Mindy. This summer was the liveliest one yet..." She stopped, her small face reflecting shock as she realized her brother's death was the reason there were extra people at Morania. Shock crumpled into grief and Claudia began to cry. Nancy put her arms around her.

"Delayed reaction," Mindy said softly to Nancy, "I knew it would have to come out sometime. Claud has been so brave, holding it all in, and trying to fool everyone, herself included, by being bold and brassy. The truth is, she's as sensitive and soft as Greg inside, and she adored her brother." She led Claudia into the bathroom. "Cry it out," she said. "You'll feel better."

Nancy was still standing holding her swimsuit when Mindy reappeared alone. "Can't always judge a book by its cover, can you?" asked Greg's cousin with a smile.

The two waited until the sobs in the bathroom quieted, and after a while, Claudia's little face, still wearing a woebegone expression peeked around the door. Again Nancy went to her and put her arms around her. "I've made no plans about Morania at all," she said, "but I'd never evict you. You will be welcome here as long as you want. Now, no more serious talk. Let's go see what we can do to help."

For once there was no snappy comeback from Greg's sister and Nancy missed it.

The three went out to the pool area taking coffee and doughnuts with them. Rosa was very much in control of her small crew, whether up on a ladder directing the hanging of lanterns or at ground level setting up wrought iron tables and chairs for the dinner to be served on the patio. She explained that Maria, one of the Whitelaw maids, would be over tonight to serve. Brent was setting up a stereo and Fred and Scott were outlining an area for poolside dancing by the placement of citronella candles.

"Rosa, you're incredible," Nancy marveled." You could be a professional party-giver the way you're organizing everything."

Rosa beamed. "I like to do it. Greg always said I made fantasies into reality with my magic."

Claudia piped up, "He also said you often couldn't tell the difference between the two."

Ordinarily, Nancy would have felt like smacking her, but for once she was glad to see Claudia playing her characteristic role. She must be feeling better.

"Grow up, Claudia," Rosa responded without rancor. "Let's get ready for tonight. This may be the last time we're all together at Morania."

It seemed to Nancy they were all looking at her with thinly veiled questions in their eyes.

CHAPTER 24

▼

The day passed quickly and with all the activity going on, Nancy managed to forget about the ugly vinyl letters on the brown cardboard for long periods at a time. She, Mindy, Claudia, and Rosa worked together in such harmony it was impossible to believe any of them could be implicated. This helped raise Nancy's spirits, and she began to look forward to tonight's festivities in a way she had previously thought impossible.

At four o'clock John arrived carrying a small satchel, which Nancy assumed was his beachwear. "Hi everyone," he greeted them, his eyes taking in the transformed pool area before resting for a moment on Nancy. Nancy tried to read his expression. Had he taken the warning? She couldn't tell, but his solid form made her feel more secure; at least until she made herself remember that his name was on her suspect list, too.

Rosa glanced at her watch. "If you're here, John, it must be time we ladies got ready."

"You're not going to change before dinner are you?" Brent leaned against the cabana surveying the girls with a smile on his face. They were a bedraggled bunch. Rosa, as usual, looked adorable although she had cobwebs in her hair, a smudge on her nose, and perspiration spots on her purple playsuit. Mindy had spilled chlorine as evidenced by the white patches down her tee shirt and jeans. Her bare feet were filthy. Claudia had helped in the kitchen and had food coloring on her fingers. Her hair was damp at the forehead, and one pigtail was coming undone. Nancy's slacks had lost their crispness, her tee shirt felt clammy as it clung to the contours of her body, and her hair had lost most of the pins that held it in place, so it stuck out untidily in all directions.

"We might just freshen up a trifle," Mindy said soberly, which made them all laugh. The girls separated themselves from the group, and made their way through the house and to their rooms, Rosa going along with Claudia.

When they rejoined, about forty-five minutes later, they were as transformed as the pool area. Rosa wore a multicolored long skirt over her bikini bottoms, Grecian style sandals laced up her ankles, with the hot pink bikini top completing her ensemble. She had pinned a large pink flower in her shiny black hair. Nancy also used the top part of her suit, though it was attached, as the top of her costume, but she had a white mini skirt over the bottom. She wore white ankle socks trimmed with jade colored ribbon run through white lace with her flat slip-on shoes. Her golden hair was in a French braid that hung down her back, tied with the same fluorescent trimming as her socks. Mindy wore a canary yellow tee shirt dress that showed the outlines of her swimsuit underneath, with yellow thong sandals. Claudia wore the same type outfit in green. "Went shopping together," she explained. They all carried bags with towels, dry clothes, and accessories.

Claudia's eyes were fixed on Nancy's straw bag. "I swear something moved in that thing," she said.

"Really? What could it have been?" Nancy deadpanned and reached into the depths of her bag and lifted out Shammy. She had twined small artificial flowers around the cat's collar, and as Shammy stretched and purred, she seemed to be as pleased with her appearance as the rest of the girls. "She's been locked out of my room all day, and insisted she wanted to come with me. I thought maybe she'd stay in the cabana as I know she won't like the pool area."

They admired the cat and each other, and chatting gaily made their way to the bathhouse to stow their gear. Nancy chose an upper cubicle, but Shammy dived into the same bottom one he'd been in the night before. "Okay, you scamp. It's terribly unhandy, but if that's the one you're determined to have, I guess I can change." She was about to move to the lower compartment, when Rosa blocked her way.

"What are you doing? That's my cubicle." Rosa quickly put her own things in the compartment and Shammy settled on top of them purring and kneading.

They stood there, the camaraderie shattered. Rosa's large luminous eyes looked wild again for a second, as they sought Claudia. "Greg gave me this locker, didn't he?" she demanded.

So that was it. "Yes-yes, he did and nobody's ever fought you for it. You gotta admit it isn't in the most desirable location. Who wants to lie on the floor to find their lipstick? Greg said it would sorta even things up, cuz even without lipstick, you look better than the rest of us."

Rosa smiled at the memory, then said, "Sorry Nancy. Guess I overreacted with all my claim of ownership."

Nancy understood, and was glad the awkward moment was over.

Dinner was enchanting, served on the patio. It was still very warm on this June evening. The birds twittered and the bees droned. John maneuvered to sit across from Nancy and he caught her attention and mouthed the words, "Don't worry. It's okay."

"Who?" Nancy blurted out, but John shook his head warningly, and asked politely for the butter.

It must have been Claudia after all, Nancy decided, and was glad it was nothing more serious.

After Maria, cleared the dishes and moved the tables out of the way, Brent turned on the stereo, and the dancing began. Nancy declined to dance with Brent and each of the other males in turn, including Ben Moran, preferring instead to sit and watch. She cuddled on a lounge, wrapping her arms around her slight body, and allowed herself the luxury of remembering; remembering other times, other music, other dancing with other arms wrapped around her, arms that belonged to Greg. For once, her memories brought more pleasure than pain, though pain was always at the perimeter of her feelings waiting to take over if given the chance.

Some of the dancers would drop out for a swim, then return to dance again. One by one each of them (except John, whom she was dying to talk to) dropped by to sit on the end of Nancy's lounge and chat before rejoining one activity or another. Nancy reveled in the understanding these friends and relatives of Greg displayed. They didn't coax her to join in the dancing, nor did they make any demands on her in conversation. They were just there making her feel a part of the group, a part of Greg, a part of them. For the first time she felt like she belonged.

She was surprised at how much she would miss Scott and Fred, but now that she'd stopped blaming them for what happened, she saw them for the immature, but fun-loving and basically good-hearted young men that they were.

Ben came over and after shifting from foot to foot, said "I'm sorry about the other night. There had been so much going on that I've gotten a bit gun-shy when it comes to discussing serious matters. I don't want to leave you with the impression that I begrudge you Morania. It's fitting that it goes to you. Everything will work out. You'll see."

"Thanks," Nancy replied, watching him fidget with his pipe. She hoped that he was sincere; that this wasn't an elaborate cover-up for deep-seated resentment.

John's words, 'don't worry. It's okay,' reassured her. "I'm not planning to live here," she said.

But Ben Moran wasn't paying attention to what she said. His mouth gaped at he stared toward the house, where a stunning woman in a black sarong was making her way toward the pool. "Mother," he gasped.

I thought it was about time I started acting a bit more neighborly, and a bit more like family," she said directly to Ben. "Losing Greg makes me realize how little time any of us may have. We've both been stubborn, but I'm going to end this feud right now. We're very different, Ben, but you're my son, and I love you. Can't you accept that?"

Ben turned away trying to hide his emotions, then turned back and hugged Amelia. "It hasn't been your fault," he said. "I've been a darned fool. I can never make it up to my son, but I can try to make it up to you."

Claudia and Mindy, unaware of what was happening, bounded up. "Grannyam," they shouted hugging and kissing Amelia. But Nancy saw the warm look she and Ben exchanged over their heads, and felt a warm glow inside herself.

Amelia was the most popular person there. She danced with all the males, and swam in the pool, and was surrounded by two or three people all the time. Nancy was glad she was never alone, for it eliminated the need to tell her she'd lost Greg's letters. She felt good Amelia was there, however, and found a strange solace in watching this woman with Greg's face and mannerisms. She knew if he'd been with them, he'd have been as popular as his grandmother.

Once it was dusk, Rosa lit the lanterns, and a card game was installed at one of the tables, but players exchanged seats with one another, as often as they exchanged partners when dancing. Nancy wandered over and watched for a while, but she didn't know the game and she didn't play. She ate some hors d'oeuvres and wandered back to her lounge. It was a very subdued party due to the circumstances, but it was pleasant and probably good for everybody.

As dusk deepened to dark, Rosa announced a new game. She had two hundred fifty pennies in a jug, which she tossed by handfuls into the pool. They were to dive for them, and the person who retrieved the most was to get tickets for two for dinner at the Captain's Table. Everyone was to play. Even the poorer swimmers had a chance, for she had flung pennies in the shallow end as well. To make the game more difficult, the pool and patio lights and lanterns would all be turned out once the contestants were ready.

Nancy didn't feel like participating. She had sipped some wine, and was enjoying a lazy evening surrounded by happier people than she'd been around since Greg died. Still, she didn't want to be a spoil sport, so when she caught

Rosa looking at her questioningly, she undid her miniskirt and removed her socks and shoes,

"You resemble a sea nymph," said John from the shallow end of the pool, where he stood. Nancy wondered if anyone besides her realized that he couldn't swim.

They all lined up around the pool, and Nancy was glad to see that Ruth Whitelaw stood by John at the shallow end. Otherwise, she would have done so rather than see him alone.

The lights went out and in total darkness the game began. The pool was a mass of squirming giggling bodies. It was a moonless night, and there was no way to see the coins. One had to dive to the bottom, then feel around hoping to hit pay dirt before running into someone. Several times Nancy reached out only to feel floating hair or worse still a warm body, which she couldn't identify as male or female, let alone who it belonged to.

She tried to find an open space, took a deep breath and dove to the bottom. This time she found coins. She grabbed up as many as she could before her lungs were aching for air, and she felt the presence of several other swimmers in the same area. Needing oxygen she pushed off, but before she could break the surface her head was given a mighty push back downwards. She swam to her right and tried again with the same results. There were two or three other swimmers around her, but though she thrashed around, no one got the message of distress she was trying to signal. The more she panicked and struggled the more oxygen she was using. She forced herself to stop struggling, took a sharp turn left and pushed upwards. The jolt to her head pushed her violently downward again. It was hard to think as she began losing consciousness. One thought did go through her mind. Somewhere she'd read that drowning was a beautiful way to die. This didn't seem beautiful.

She was bobbing up and down, not of her own volition; merely floating up and being pushed down like a yo-yo. Only semi-conscious now, she heard her name far far away. "Nancy. Nancy." Perhaps it was God. It was beginning to be beautiful.

CHAPTER 25

▼

Suddenly her head was above water, and she was coughing, sputtering, and retching. Hands reached out to help her. The lights came on and she sprawled on the cool cement with Mindy beside her and John right behind Mindy. Turning Nancy's head to the side Mindy pushed on her abdomen, and more water spewed from her mouth.

She could tell they were all gathered around her, but she kept her eyes tightly closed. She didn't want to see them. One of them had tried to drown her. She could feel Mindy checking her carotid pulse. She knew it was all right for she could feel her heart thumping wildly.

"What happened?" It sounded like Scott.

"I don't know. I just knew she was down for too long, and I started calling her name." That was John.

"How could you tell in the dark?" Ben's voice was unmistakable.

"Her hair bow. It had that plastic fluorescent material in it, and it glowed in the dark."

"And you kept track of it?" Amelia sounded as incredulous as Nancy felt.

"When it was above water," John answered simply.

"Can you hear me? Do you feel any better?" Mindy spoke softly in her ear.

"Yes, yes." Nancy answered. "Get me away from here." She was shaking all over. Mindy covered her with a beach towel and slid another beneath her.

"What did she say? How did it happen?" Isabel's voice sounded as shaky as Nancy was feeling.

"She didn't say. I think we should take her to her room."

Nancy opened her eyes. Everyone looked upset and worried, but Isabel Moran and Steve Whitelaw looked the worst. They both had identical white drawn faces. But, did they look guilty? She couldn't tell.

Rosa recovered first. "Thank God, you're all right," she said. She put her arm around Nancy's shoulder, hugging her and helping her sit up. "I'll divert them, so you can take care of her," she said in an aside to John and Mindy. She stood up and eyed the group. "Well, let's count those pennies," she said, "and let's do it over here away from Nancy. She needs air."

Most of the crowd followed Rosa though the Morans and Amelia stayed behind with John and Mindy.

"That was a scare," Amelia smiled at Nancy, 'but at least you're looking better every minute."

"Can we help?" Isabel still was deathly pale.

Ben gave her an awkward pat. "I think you should stay on dry land," he said. "You and water don't seem to mix."

"She's okay now," Mindy said," but she needs to get to her room and rest quietly for a while." Her no nonsense voice predicted the good nurse she would become. "I'll take her," she added.

Nancy agreed gratefully as Mindy and John helped her to her feet. "I want you both to go with me," she said, "but the bathhouse first, please."

"We can get your things," John said, and Nancy noticed he already had her clothes from the lounge.

"No, I want to go," she said. In the cabana, she wiped up a little, and put on her warm-up suit. Still, she shook. She grabbed her bag and started toward Mindy, then remembered Shammy. Bending down to look in the bottom cubicle caused another bout of nausea. She straightened up slowly, and since the little cat was still contentedly sleeping, she decided to leave her alone.

On the way to her room, both Mindy and John asked her what had happened.

"I don't remember. I guess I blacked out." Nancy knew well what had happened, but she had no intention of letting anyone know she knew. It might be dangerous. It also might be dangerous to be alone with anyone. That's why she insisted that both Mindy and John accompany her. She didn't seriously believe either of them was involved, but she wasn't taking any chances. She hadn't surfaced that far from the shallow end where John stood, and he might have been able to reach her for all she knew. He certainly had been able to identify her in the dark. As far as Mindy went, she had no idea where she was at the time Nancy was being dribbled like a basketball in the pool.

"A cramp, maybe?" Mindy persisted.

"Maybe. I just don't know." She wanted to get to her room, and lock the door behind her. Then, she'd feel safe.

They finally left her alone with many admonitions. Gratefully, Nancy locked the door behind them. She still felt cold and shaky, but the hot bath prescribed by Mindy was unappealing. She'd had enough water to last for a good long while.

She settled for a wash-up at her bathroom sink, and a pair of foot pajamas that said, 'My heart belongs to Greg Moran', a gift from the same. To complete her ensemble, she donned his faithful oversized robe.

She cuddled in a chair under a comforter until she felt warm, and the major trembling had ceased. Then, she walked out on the balcony, and stood staring toward the pool area, her fingers hooked in the beltless loops of the robe. The plasticized ribbon she'd used to hold back her still wet braid slid to the floor, glowing on the darkened balcony. She bent to retrieve it, experiencing only slight nausea. Suddenly, something clicked in her mind.

For a long moment she remained motionless, afraid to do what she must. She did not want to go back to the pool area. She did not want to leave the haven of her room. But there was something peculiar out there; something she needed to find out about.

Determinedly, she picked up the newly emptied straw bag. If she met anyone, she'd say she was going to get Shammy. If she met anyone—oh dear, the thought filled her with terror.

Still, she unlocked the door, the click of the inside lock sounding as loud to her ears as a gunshot. As she silently opened the door, there was nothing to greet her but darkness. Darkness would be her ally, she told herself; a cloak to cover her as she went about her business; to hide her from the one who wanted her dead until she could return safely to her room.

She slipped into the hall, carefully locking the door behind her and depositing the key in the straw bag. She wanted no one waiting for her when she returned. Her pajama covered feet made no sound as she made her way to the stairs. Darkness is my ally, she kept telling herself as she padded down the stairs into more blackness below. Darkness had also been the ally of her would-be murderer, she told herself, and if it hadn't been for the stupid little bow in her hair and John, she might be dead by now. Another thought struck her. The bow must have identified her for whoever kept her bobbing in the water, for they would be able to see no better than anyone else. Then, it couldn't have been premeditated. She found it all confusing. She wished she knew what John had found out. She wished she had something tangible. Then, she could call the police.

At the foot of the stairs, Nancy stopped. She heard voices coming from the kitchen. The trembling she was doing now was from fear, not shock. Her heartbeat began to slow as she listened. Mrs. Whitelaw was talking to the maid from their estate.

"A very nice job," she was saying. "It's good of you to put in this extra time, Maria."

Nancy didn't listen further. She made a beeline through the house and out towards the pool. The closer she got, the more frightened she became. She peeked around the gate. The only lights on the patio were the lanterns and candles since the bright lights were turned off. Could she just get through the gate and into the cabana without being seen? No one seemed to be looking her way. The decision as to when to go was taken from her, for she could hear Mrs. Whitelaw approaching from the rear.

Without another thought, she slipped through the gate and dashed into the bathhouse, leaning against the wall to catch her breath, and peering through the crack made by the door hinge. What she saw frightened her anew for Ruth Whitelaw was coming directly toward the bathhouse door.

Before she could move, the door was pushed into her face, and the light clicked on. Nancy stood where she was holding her breath. After a few minutes, heels clicked towards her and the light went off. She was alone once again.

Without hesitation, Nancy moved quickly to the opposite wall and knelt by the bottom cubicle. She removed the startled cat, who began rubbing against her squatted legs, and then she proceeded to remove the contents. It was completely empty except for the tiny something she thought she'd seen earlier, that which had prompted this visit. Grabbing it in both hands, she tugged but it would not come. She tugged harder and the plywood base lifted out releasing the trapped article. As she peered into the dark hole, she was not overly surprised. Silently, she began filling her basket.

CHAPTER 26

▼

"Thank you, Mr. Flaherty. You won't be sorry." Nancy was sitting across from the newspaperman, beaming happily. She'd just landed her first job.

"I don't expect I will," he said, 'but remember this is a tough business, and it takes a tough cat to survive in it."

"Then, I'll just have to be a 'tough cat,' won't I?" she asked lightly.

He examined the fragile girl in the pale pink silk suit, with the red gold curls cascading down her back. "It may take a bit of doing," he said mildly.

"I'll do whatever it takes," she promised. "Thank you again. I'll see you Monday morning."

As she left the building and folded her long legs into the compact car she'd borrowed from Mindy, she couldn't help smiling to herself. Tough, did he say? Well, if surviving made you tough, then she ought to be as hard as nails. Little did Mr. Flaherty know of what she'd been through.

She put the car in gear and drove the few blocks to the furnished apartment she'd rented this morning. She wanted one more peek at it before driving back to Morania. It was tiny, but perfect. Just looking at the rose and white striped chintz sofa and the dear white wooden rocker made her happy. The kitchen was the size of an average bathroom, but everything was compact and built for efficiency. There was a white counter dividing it from the living room with two bar stools drawn up before two pink placemats. The bedroom and bath completed her new home, and after another contented look, she closed and locked the door.

Wonder what Mike Flaherty thinks it would take to toughen a person up, she wondered on the way back to Morania. The loss of a loved one," she'd suffered that one four times over, what with her parents, grandmother, and Greg. Fear that her husband really loved someone else? She'd worried about that for a period of time. Theft of personal property? Another curve fortune (or should she say misfortune?) had thrown her way. Fear, for one's personal safety? She hadn't felt very safe out on the river with no oars. Feeling of not being wanted? How many times she'd felt that at Morania. BEWARE, the sign had said, MORANIA WILL NEVER BE YOURS. Fear for one's life? Bingo again, Mr. Flaherty.

She thought back to that night when she'd been so afraid. Once she'd gotten back to her room with her basket and Shammy, she'd dumped everything out on her bed. Shammy looked interested, and began batting at the article Nancy had tugged at, and in so doing, discovered the secret cache. "You are a smart cat, Shammy," Nancy said, "for it was really you who found this." She reached down and picked up the belt to Greg's robe then examined the rest of her find. Everything was there—her marriage certificate, a hacksaw, a small can of plastic wood, Amelia's brown manila envelope with Greg's letters in it, and several sheets of plastic vinyl letters, some with letters missing.

She felt sick and unable to explain what it all meant. Rosa? She and Rosa had come to an understanding. They were friends. Besides, Rosa had nothing to gain with Nancy out of the picture. She remembered the beautiful girl hugging her at poolside and diverting the rest of them so Nancy could escape to her room. She thought of the way they'd sobbed their hearts out, of Rosa's changed manner after that; no longer sullen but sunny. Why? Why? She asked herself. What wasn't she seeing?

Later, the why began to unfold, but that was only after she'd unsealed the envelope, and begun to read the stack of letters which Greg had sent to Amelia, a stack that dated back to his first year at Rutgers.

It seemed that Rosa had been a beautiful baby, but as she grew into a toddler, she began banging her head against the wall. She would also rock back and forth making a strange humming sound and paying no attention to what went on around her. The Whitelaws took her from specialist to specialist, and sometime in this period, the distraught Ruth had a breakdown, and had to be hospitalized. A tentative diagnosis of autism was made in Rosa's case, and treatment of a sort instituted, though doctors held out little hope for a complete recovery. (Nancy looked up autism in her dictionary and found it to be an emotional disturbance characterized by morbid self-absorption and inability to relate to other people, usually diagnosed in early childhood.) They said it was very difficult to treat and only about a third of such children grow up to be functioning adults. Even then, they frequently had difficulty with normal human relations.

Mrs. Whitelaw, in the meantime, returned home, but her nerves remained fragile ever after. Rosa continued with her therapists twice a week, and then miraculously, she also recovered. Growing more beautiful every day, she began to interact with her environment and those who peopled it.

All during this period, Isabel had been the bulwark for the disintegrating Whitelaws, taking much of the responsibility for Rosa during Ruth's absence even though Greg was a small boy, and she was pregnant with, then had baby Claudia. Claudia was left with her nurse, but Greg usually went along with his mother to the Whitelaws and was greatly affected by the tot and her problems.

Rosa seemed a perfectly normal delightful child after that until she became a teenager, which was about when Greg began college. Perhaps, because he didn't see her as frequently, he was aware of changes in her that no one else noticed at first. During this period she did not display her autistic behavior, and, in fact, was perfectly normal most of the time. At other times she seemed to break with reality and live in her own fantasy world. She went through a period of stealing inconsequential items and squirreling them away. Another time she believed the handsome man who drove the school bus was a prince escaped from a foreign country come to marry her.

Steve Whitelaw turned to Isabel with his worries once again, and they both tried to shield Ruth, for they worried about another breakdown. They had Rosa see the family doctor, a kindly fellow who knew her history, but he found nothing to be alarmed about. "All teenagers act strangely," he said.

It took Nancy a long time to glean all this information, for it was not the main topic in his letters to his grandmother, merely a paragraph here, a sentence there, but a continual thread that kept reappearing until Nancy was able to weave the fabric of the story. His more recent letters were mostly about Nancy, herself, but even they mentioned several times that when he received his trust, he was going to donate money for research so kids like Rosa could be helped. At last, Nancy understood what Amelia meant when she said she might change her mind about the money once she read Greg's letters.

She also understood why Steve Whitelaw and Isabel Moran were so often together, and she felt ashamed of her own interpretation. She could also guess why they'd both been so upset and pale when the letters were missing and tonight at the pool. They were afraid Rosa was involved.

This was confirmed when she talked to the two of them the next day. John Stacy had already asked Isabel about the sign, and Isabel had mentioned that Rosa was going through a stage where she did silly things and there was a good chance she might have done it. As Rosa had never harmed or even tried to harm anyone before, she didn't elaborate and John was contented with the explanation. Steve and Isabel worried about what they should do, but decided it could wait until after the party. "Please don't think too harshly of us or of her," Steve begged. "We were hoping against hope that it wasn't true, but even if it was, we never dreamed she'd hurt you. I'll see that she gets treatment, even if it means that she has to be locked away." His voice broke. "My poor little girl," he said.

"Rosa didn't mean to hurt me," she said. "She was living in another world at that moment. She needs treatment, yes, but she can get it without being locked up." If she pressed charges, the law might decide differently, but she would never do it. This poor beautiful childhood friend of Greg's had been through enough, and so had the Whitelaws and Isabel. She made sure they understood what she was saying.

As she pulled Mindy's car into the circular drive at Morania, she felt Greg's presence beside her and she sensed his approval. He'd be pleased that Ben, Isabel. and Claudia would continue to use Morania as their summer home, even though Ben insisted on paying a minimal rent; pleased that she would spend part of her summers with them for they were her family now; pleased that Claudia would start college in the fall, where she planned to study Journalism like her idol, Nancy; pleased that Mindy and Brent were drawn together over their concern for Rosa; pleased that John Stacy was investigating how to best put a large chunk of his inheritance to work for Rosa and against autism and she was sure he'd be delighted about her new job and apartment.

In her mind she could hear him talking to Mike Flaherty. "Not tough enough? Why, I'd put this little kitten in the ring with any of your cub reporters, and wager she'd come out the winner any day. After all she studied at the Pussy-cat Lounge. What better place to learn to be a tough cat?"

And what about your own feelings, she asked herself. What about John Stacy? She knew the answer. She wanted to live in her apartment for the time being with Greg's little cat, Shammy, and with Greg, even if it was only his spirit or memory. As for the future, who could say? She did know that whoever or whatever the future might bring, Greg would be part of her forever. It was a nice thought.

THE END

CUSTOMER PROFILE

Judy Conlin
2774 Tallavana Trail
Havana, FL 32333
850-539-8062

jconlin@inetw2.net

Royalty Participant and Primary Contact-Judy Conlin, Author

978-0-595-40440-7
0-595-40440-5